MW01644896

My Forever Love

- *A Novel* -

Marilynn J. Harris

Cottage Publishing

Cottage Publishing
Boise, Idaho
www.marilynnjharris.com

First published by Cottage Publishing: 10-6-2022

ISBN: 9798356900365

Printed in the United States of America

For information or to order more books please visit our website:
www.marilynnjharris.com

Or Contact:
Cottage Publishing
8530 W Targee Street
Boise, ID 83709

Books by Marilynn J. Harris

The Moon Mountain Series

On Top of Moon Mountain: book one

Beyond the Idaho Mountains: book two

Return to Terror Mountain: book three

The Enigma Series

Enigma Fire: book one

Enigma Winds: book two

Enigma Sun: book three

The Magic Christmas Kite

Song of the River

Eyewitness Report

Through the Eyes of Desmond

Dedication:

To my loving husband, Darrell, who taught me about forever love. We got married as teenagers, and we had to learn that a successful marriage requires falling in love many times, but always with the same person. Through births, and deaths and illness too, somehow, we did survive. Through prayer and grace and diligence we kept our vows alive.

1 Thessalonians 5:16-18

Rejoice always, pray continually, give thanks in all circumstances; for this is God's will for you in Christ Jesus.

Table of Contents

One
Church Camp

My eternal love story actually began when I was only thirteen years old. That is the year that I first met my forever love. No matter how long I live, I will never forget that day. I was in my church youth group listening to Pastor Jim Franklin tell us about the upcoming church camp, when the most handsome boy I had ever seen in my life, timidly walked into our junior high youth group, and sat down next to my brother and his friends.

I was at that age where I had just started noticing boys, and there were plenty of handsome young men in our church to choose from. But this new boy, Andrew was unlike any other boy that I had ever met. He was tall and slender with soft wispy blond hair, a smooth tanned skin, and huge innocent bright blue eyes.

Of course, this was only his first time to our church group, and I did not know him, but he just seemed different. He was reserved, polite, and undeniably mature. "Our church was large, and we had a huge youth group, and we had new people almost every week, so why was I so attracted to this boy?" I asked myself.

He acted so grown-up compared to the other boys, and I couldn't stop watching him. When he glanced my way and smiled, my heart sincerely skipped a beat. "Is there such a thing as love at first sight," I thought to myself. "I was only thirteen years old, what did I know?" I rationalized. "All I knew about love at this point in my life, was the unconditional love of my parents, my brother, my grandparents and my cousins."

After youth group was over, everyone gathered around a large table and drank punch, ate cookies, and talked about going to camp in two weeks. This would be the first church camp for most of us, and we could hardly wait to go. Year after year we had watched as the older kids got on the bus, and traveled 90 miles away for 5 days of fun, fellowship, and freedom; and this year it was our turn.

As confident and outgoing as I was, I could not get myself to walk over and talk to the new-comer in the group, but he immediately hit it off with my twin brother, Keith. I could see them across the room laughing and having a great time, so at least he was talking to someone.

School had just finished for the school year, and now my brother and I were officially in the eighth grade. We felt so grown up. We had finally arrived. I was very close with my twin brother Keith; he was my best friend. I often think that a person has a lot more confidence in themselves when they have a twin to share their life with. You are never alone; you continually have someone there to let you know that you are alright. Keith was only four minutes older than me, but he never let me forget that I was his 'little' sister. He was always there to protect me from the world.

Keith and I came from a very strong Christian family. Our mother was a children's Sunday school teacher and our father was an elder in the church. Going to church was all we had ever known. It was a large part of our lives. From the time we were little, it was just normal to attend Sunday school every Sunday, and when you got old enough you joined the youth group, and you went to summer camp.

Sunday morning during church I noticed a sophisticated older white-haired lady sitting in the pew across from our family. It was odd that I would even notice her, because she was old enough to be my grandma, but I noticed her because of her radiant smile. She was literally beaming from ear to ear as she sang praises to the Lord.

She seemed so excited to be in church, and she completely ignored every other person around her, she just kept focused on worshipping her God. She was dressed elegantly in a dark-purple knit suit with a matching purple feathered hat, matching shoes and she wore delicate little white gloves. With her beautiful white-hair, she was absolutely stunning.

I do not think I had ever seen this lady in our church before, but she was so intriguing I couldn't take my eyes of off her. Even at thirteen years old my heart was touched by her genuine deep conviction and Love for the Lord. It was inspiring to watch her, because she was so joyful and confident. I could tell she was wealthy by the way she was dressed and the way she carried herself, yet she was so focused that I knew she wasn't at church to impress anyone; she was there to praise the Lord.

As I watched her, a strange feeling came over me. Although, I had gone to church all my life I thought the Bible stories were for young people like me. I rarely paid attention to the older people in the church, but I could tell this attractive white-haired lady loved the Bible stories, and the Lord just as much as I did.

It was like a light-bulb went off in my head, and I realized that the sermon that Pastor Bill Jamison was preaching pertained to all of us, and I had never really thought of it before. I always applied everything I heard to me and my family, but this beautiful white-haired lady truly opened my eyes. Her entire being expressed wealth and elegance, and yet she put God before anything else. It was strange because she made such a strong Christian impression on me as I observed her from across the church, and she had no idea I was even watching her.

When the church service was over and our family was walking out, I once again noticed the beautiful white-haired lady as she was leaving the church. She had a nice-looking older gentleman on one side of her, who was also very well-dressed, but guiding her along on the other side was that handsome new stranger Andrew, who had come to our youth group the week before.

As our family walked by, Andrew looked up and confidently smiled at me and nodded hello. My heart instantly skipped a few beats, but I timidly smiled back at him and shyly mouthed hello. "The stunning well-dressed lady must be his grandma," I thought.

Over the next two weeks, we planned and impatiently waited for the day to arrive when we could get on the bus and we could travel off to our first adventure of summer camp. I was so excited I could think of nothing else, but going to camp. Finally, everything was packed and organized and we hugged our mom and dad goodbye and began climbing aboard the modern Greyhound bus.

I sat with my best friend Margaret, and my friends Caryn and Carolyn sat in the seats behind us. My friends Diane and Mary sat in the seat in front of us, and the seats directly across from me were Connie and Suzanne, and Ruth and MaryEllen. We soon discovered if we stood up, we could see over the top of the tall seats and easily talk to each other. The bus seats were soft and comfortable and we were so full of excitement everyone on the bus chattered with joy.

Suddenly, I had mixed emotions as the bus doors began to close, and I waved one last goodbye to my parents from the bus window. I felt like crying as I watched my mom and dad slowly disappear out of sight as our bus drove away and left them standing in the church parking lot.

For some reason, I didn't feel as confident about going to church camp as I had in the past few days. Maybe I wasn't as grown up as I thought. I loved my mom and dad and I had never been away from home before. I wanted to stop the bus and shout, "I changed my mind, I need to stay home. I can go next year." I could hardly catch my breath, I was so disturbed, but I knew it was too late. I was trapped inside this enormous bus, with the rest of the youth group, and like it or not we were quickly being swept away from our families, and we were on our way to church camp for five long days.

I just sat quietly and said nothing, I didn't want everyone to think I was a baby. I slowly glanced around to see where my twin brother Keith was sitting. When I spotted him a few rows back, he instantly smiled and gave me the thumbs up sign. Keith knew me well, he probably guessed I was already homesick, but just seeing him smile reassured me that everything would be O.K.

For the next few miles nobody spoke, maybe my friends were having second thoughts too. We all just sat quietly in our huge bus seats, and looked out the window. Occasionally, we whispered to the friend sitting next to us, but most of the bus was very quiet.

All of a sudden, one the boys in the back of the bus hit me in the side of the head with a small wad of paper. That was the end of the silence. You could hear giggles from all around the bus. As I turned to see where the paper wad had come from, I saw my friend Johnny Johnson waving and grinning from ear to ear. Johnny was always teasing me about something. He was in several of my classes at school, and he often carried some of my books and walked me down the hall in between classes. He was very tall and thin, with thick black hair and deep brown eyes. He was so cute with his silly grin and his funny jokes. He always made me laugh. Johnny was also a good friend of my brother.

Within a few minutes, one of the other boys stood up and hollered out my name. I smiled as I saw my sweet friend Mark Jamison waving to me from the back of the bus. Mark was the son of our Pastor, Bill Jamison. Mark had been a friend of mine since kindergarten.

"Oh Kathryn, Are you alright?" Mark sincerely asked as if he were coming to my rescue. Before I could answer, Nick, stood up and tried to hit Mark in the side of the head with another wad of paper, but Mark ducked down and the wad of paper hit Roger instead. That was the end of the peaceful bus ride. Paper began flying in every direction until Pastor Jim had had enough and he put a stop to our fiasco.

The good-natured silliness made me relax and I realized, I wasn't alone. I was going to camp with all my friends. When things finally calmed down, Margaret and I talked and laughed all the way to camp. We had been best friends since we were in the nursery at our church. Our moms and dads had been friends since before we were born. Her birthday was three months before Keith and I were born. Margaret was intelligent, calm, and gracious. She was the kind of friend that made you feel better, just by being there. She always had just the right answer to any problem. It was Margaret who taught me to pray about everything.

My brother and I were born on Friday the 13th, but the 13th was never unlucky for us, our lives had always been blessed. Keith was born first and he was named Keith Matthew Hartford, and I was named Kathryn Elizabeth Hartford. Our father's name was Matthew Hartford and our mother's name was Elizabeth Hartford, that is where we got our middle names.

Our father worked for a large cooperation with outlets all over the United States. My brother and I were born in a quaint little town called Arlington, Massachusetts about six miles northwest of Boston. My parents thought it was the ideal place to raise a family and enjoy the beauty and history of our Nation. Arlington had the personal charm of a small-town community, and yet a few miles up the road was the illustrious town of Boston, Massachusetts.

Boston, is the most populous city of the commonwealth of Massachusetts. It is the 21st most popular city in the country. Boston is best known for its baked beans, Fenway Park, Boston Crème pie, and The Boston Marathon. Many people think Boston is the best city in America; maybe even the entire world.

The company our father worked for was in Boston so we traveled into the Boston area a couple of times a month. We never tired of the delicious restaurants, the wonderful museums, the walking tours, Beacon Hill, Back Bay, and North End Little Italy.

Boston was a combination of a wonderland of enchantment, and strolling back through history. We enjoyed the Bunker Hill Museum, the Mystic Aquarium, and the 1837 city park with the wonderful Swan boat rides. My brother and I both felt we were lucky to be born in Arlington, Massachusetts and to live so close to Boston.

We lived in a beautiful old restored mansion-type house that had been built in the nineteen-hundreds. Our mother had always appreciated the architecture of the old houses in Arlington, and when they decided to buy a home, she knew just the house she wanted; she had been admiring it for years. To her, the old three-story stately home was a dream come true. She could see beyond the massive expense and the numerous hours of restoration and remodeling.

My mother was a professional decorator, and she had helped restore many of the notable houses around the Massachusetts area. She told us when they first purchased our old house all she could see was a beautiful part of Arlington's history. She could only envision a stately 1900's home, on a quiet street in downtown Arlington with our family's name on the mailbox.

Our charming home sat on the back of the property with a long private sidewalk that led up to the wrap-around over-sized front porch. The entire house was surrounded by manicured thick green grass, flowers, and shrubs. Our enormous front yard was enclosed by a decorative black iron fence and there were several large Red Maple trees scattered throughout the yard. The house was painted a light yellow with white trim, and it was magnificent. It was one of the most imposing houses in Arlington. I loved our house almost as much as my mother did.

Our parents had purchased the home two years before we were born. They said when they bought it, it was greatly in need of restoration. By the time we were born, our mother had completed the renovation and she had transformed it into an amazing three-story mansion. Our home had five large bedrooms, a beautiful over-sized remodeled kitchen, a huge front-room, and a sunny sitting room. My mother was a wonderful pianist, and she had a small baby grand piano over in one corner of the sitting room. Keith and I started taking piano lessons when we were only five years old.

The third story was a large attic room used partly for storage, but mainly for our mother's office and sewing area. When we were about four years old our mother once again started working a few hours a week, and she used the attic room as her preparation area. She had several large tables to lay out her designs and plenty of room to have her clients see what she had prepared for them. In that big room there was also three professional sewing machines, and a large office desk and two over-sized chairs. In recent years, they had also converted the area in the back of the room into a modern full-sized bathroom with a huge walk-in closet.

The attic room had a large dormer which made the room appear enormous and open. The front area had two large double glass doors opening out towards the front of the house onto a deck that extended from one end of the window to the other.

The third story was a perfect place for a workroom and office for our mother's business. She rarely had clients that came to her work area, but it was there if she needed it. She usually took all completed ideas to the client's home.

The attic room had two large doors that opened out onto the top landing with a staircase off to the right. The wide staircase angled down to the second landing, and continued down to the first floor. My parents had fully restored the beautiful massive wooden staircase to its original design. The impressive staircase elegantly weaved down through the center of the mansion to give our home a look of sophistication and unique charm.

Of course, my favorite room in the whole house was my bedroom. My mother had helped me decorate everything in pink and white ruffles. My bedroom had a large bay window that looked out onto our enormous front yard, and from my second story window I could see all the way down the street for several blocks.

Being a twin made me really appreciate my alone time. I used to sit in my window seat and read for hours and just soak in the wonderful warm sunshine. I had a big four poster bed, but the room was so large I had plenty of space for two dressers, and one complete wall with floor to ceiling book shelves and a couple of matching over-stuffed chairs. In one corner of the room, I had my huge oak desk, and my massive doll collection. Having such a joyful home and a comfortable life made it that much harder for me to leave my parents and head off to church camp; but going to church camp that year ended up being one of the greatest events of my life.

We arrived at camp around noon. We unloaded our sleeping bags and got organized in our dorm and were told we needed to go to the cafeteria to have lunch. Margaret, Carolyn, Diane, Connie, Mary, Caryn, Suzanne, MaryEllen and Ruth and I all shared one large dorm room. It was so fun having all my best friends there at camp together. The lodge where the camp was held was breathtaking. After we quickly put our things away, we headed for the cafeteria. Suddenly, I felt starved.

When we got to the cafeteria, we realized most of our other friends, from the bus were already there. They were all sitting around several long tables over by the wall. I instantly spotted my brother Keith sitting at the table with Johnny sitting on his left side and Mark sitting on his right, and Roger and Nick were sitting on the end of the table next to Johnny.

For one quick moment, my heart fluttered when I saw the handsome new guy, sitting on the other side of Mark. I quickly waved and every one of the boys at the table waved back; even my handsome new friend, Andrew.

The lunch was yummy. We had grilled cheese sandwiches, a cup of fruit salad, chips, milk, and a brownie for dessert. We quickly found an empty table and began our first day of church camp. Just as we were finishing our lunch a lady came in the cafeteria and announced that after we clean off our plates, and put our trays on the counter; we were to meet in the chapel in a half an hour.

The chapel was directly down the hall from the cafeteria, so we finished putting our trays away and headed for chapel. As we lined up to enter the chapel, we were each given a nametag with our name along with our Biblical meaning. My Nametag said, Kathryn, *pure or clear*, Margaret's nametag said, *Jewel or pearl,* Suzanne's nametag said, *lily or rose*, Carolyn's nametag said, *joy or song of happiness*. Mary's nametag said, *beloved or wished for*, Connie's said, *to be knowledgeable or steadfast.* Caryn's nametag said, *ray of light*, Ruth's nametag said, *Compassionate friend,* and Diane's said, *goddess of the moon and the hunt*.

As my friends and I were walking into the chapel sharing what each other's nametag said, my brother Keith and his friends walked up to us and started sharing what their Biblical names said. Keith's nametag said, *tactfulness, freshness, or cautiousness*. Mark shyly told me, "My nametag says, *God of War or warlike.*" Johnny proudly stated, "Mine says *Jehovah's gift.*" Roger's nametag read, *Famous spear,* and Nick's nametag read, *People's champion or conqueror of people.*

As I turned to go and sit in the chapel, I ran right into my handsome new friend Andrew. Andrew gently put his hands on both of my shoulders to stop me from bumping into him. For one quick moment, I just stood there. We were standing so close to each other that I could not move. I instinctively looked at his nametag and it said Andrew: *manly, brave, strong, courageous warrior*.

Standing that close to him, I could tell that he was at least a head taller than me, and I self-consciously glanced up and quietly mouthed, "Oh excuse me." For one second, we stared directly into each-other's eyes and just timidly smiled. I finally came to my senses and went and found the chair that Margaret had saved for me. I looked down the row to where Andrew was sitting, and he was still watching me and smiling.

When my heart stopped fluttering, I looked around and I realized that the chapel was beautiful, with its stained-glass windows and high cathedral ceilings. It had rows and rows of soft padded dark-green chairs. I closed my eyes for one second and I could just feel the presence of the Lord in that giant room.

Soon, a young pastor by the name of Pastor Stephen began to lead us in some familiar Christian hymns. Our voices sounded like angels as they echoed throughout the large building with the high ceilings. My entire being began to relax, and I instantly understood that I had made the right choice in coming to camp. Keith and I had been playing the piano for years and we both appreciated music, and I loved singing, and even at thirteen years old I knew this is where the Lord wanted me to be.

After chapel, we went into a large craft room to do a special project. We were each given a small wooden picture frame to put together, and inside we made a three-dimensional cut-out of Jesus holding a lamb and a staff. We pasted the layers on top of each other, and then attached and glued the frame together around it. We glued a small paper on the bottom of the frame that said the beginning of Psalm 23: The Lord is my shepherd; I shall not want... Our challenge for the week was to memorize the complete 23rd Psalm.

Of course, I memorized the 23rd Psalm and have carried it in my heart my entire life. I truly loved my unique picture of Jesus holding a lamb. (That small picture meant so much to me, that I kept the little cardboard image of Jesus beside my bed for many years, long after that first church camp had ended.)

That evening after dinner we had a contest between the boys and the girls. The boys all sat on one side of the room and the girls sat on the other side. Each side chose three people to represent their team. Margaret and I and a girl named Sherry were to represent the girls team. Mark, Keith, and a boy named Frank represented the boys team.

When it was our turn, we were shown a picture of a character from the Bible and ask who the person was. We won the boys 20 to 18.

Early the next morning it was time to ride the zip line. It looked a little scary because we had to climb so high up on the pole to get on it, but my friends were in line, so I got in line too. We watched as, Johnny, Keith, Mark, and Andrew went racing down to the bottom of the hill, squealing, and laughing and having a great time.

There was only one boy in front of me and then it would be my turn. The boy was someone I didn't know, he was from another church, but I felt kind of sorry for him, because he seemed really scared. He wasn't very big, and he looked absolutely terrified, but he was determined to keep up with all the other boys. All of a sudden, he leaped and he wasn't tied on properly, I stood behind him and watched in total shock as he held on for several seconds then flipped upside down, and fell to the ground. It was horrifying to be so close and watch him fall, because he fell about twenty feet to the ground.

Every one of the counselors ran to help him as he was screaming in pain. Luckily, he was talking so we knew he was not unconscious, but they immediately closed the zip line, and to this day I have never ridden a zip line. The young man named Clint was rushed to the hospital with a broken shoulder, and his arm was broken in three different places.

Everything else about the camp was so fun, at each chapel our camp director Pastor Mathews shared wonderful stories of Jesus. One morning Pastor Mathews handed out a sheet of paper for each camper to keep and look at every single day for the next three months.

We were told to hang this paper up somewhere in our house when we get home. Somewhere where we could easily see it. The hand-out said:

7 THINGS CHRISTIANS SHOULD TELL THEMSELVES EACH DAY.

1. God is my Father
2. Christ is my Savior.
3. Heaven is my home.
4. Scripture is my guide.
5. Every believer is my family.
6. The gospel is my message.
7. God's glory is my goal.

I went to bed each night full of love and praise.

During chapel on the fourth day, I was surprised to see my handsome new friend standing up in front with Pastor Mathews and Pastor Stephen. Andrew was singing and playing a guitar. He looked like a movie star. I was absolutely in awe, even more than I had been before, but as I looked around at my friends, I realized they too were in awe of this good-looking newcomer.

That night when I went to sleep, I had a strange dream: I saw Andrew and I standing together up in front of the church, and we were getting married. I woke with a start, "Was the Lord telling me that I was going to marry Andrew someday?" I had to laugh because I had never even really talked to him yet. "I wonder what his last name is?" I said to myself. I smiled as I fell back to sleep, but I never told anyone of my dream.

On Saturday, Pastor Mathews along with three other ministers did a baptismal in the river. Keith and I were both baptized and we recommitted our lives to the Lord. Over fifty other campers were baptized that day, along with my handsome guitar player, and many of my very best friends. I knew my life would never be the same again after that week at camp. Not only because of my good-looking new friend, but because of my new commitment to Jesus.

In closing chapel, many of us received a ribbon for memorizing the 23rd Psalm. Keith and I both got a ribbon, and we proudly hung ours up in our rooms when we got home from camp. We discovered that going to church camp when we were thirteen years old made an impact on our hearts that would never go away.

Two

Eighth Grade

Before we knew it, summer was over and it was once again time for school. I hadn't seen my new friend Andrew since we returned from camp. Apparently, his family had a cabin in the mountains, and they had been staying up there most of the summer.

The first day of school was exciting because many of our friends had not seen each other since school was out last year. The halls were alive with laughter and hugs. We were all so glad to see each other, and to once again be back in school.

We were anxious to find our new classes, and see how many of our old friends were in each of our classes. It was strange, but Johnny was in every one of my classes except for one. He was such a cutey, so I never minded having him around. He was handsome and funny and he made friends with everyone he met.

As I went to my English class, I spotted Andrew walking through the door in front of me. He sat down at a desk on the other side of the room. I could not help but stare, I think he was even more handsome than he was at the beginning of the summer.

Our English teacher introduced herself, she said her name was Mrs. Bingham. She said the most important thing about each of her students, was their names. So, she began to call role, and with each student she stated their first, middle and last name. it was really kind of an interesting idea to hear each student called by their entire name. She called Margaret Ann King, Kathryn Elizabeth Hartford, Keith Matthew Hartford, Johnathon Benjamin Johnson. Then came Andrew and she read; Andrew Paul Brookshire the third. "Andrew Paul Brookshire the 3rd," I repeated inside my head. "Hmmm...Kathryn Elizabeth Brookshire, that has a nice sound to it," I thought to myself as I grinned.

After class, Johnny walked up and said, "Well, Kathryn Elizabeth Hartford are you ready to go to the lunch room to have lunch?"

"That's sound great, Johnathon Benjamin Johnson," I said laughingly. We stopped by our lockers and left our books, then headed off to the lunch room with Margaret, Keith, Mark, and Carolyn.

Two weeks after school started, Keith and I had our 14th birthday. On Saturday afternoon we invited all our friends to meet us at the movies to see a double feature. We saw

'The Nutty Professor' with Jerry Lewis, and the second show was 'The Birds.'

As always, Johnny sat on one side of me and Margaret sat on the other side. Andrew, Mark, Carolyn, and Suzanne sat in the row in front of us with Keith and some of Keith's other friends. During the movie 'The Birds,' I was so scared that I held on tight to Johnny's hand and didn't let go. After the movie at the ice cream parlor, Johnny asked me if I would be his steady girlfriend. He was one of my best friends, so of course I smiled and said yes.

Having a steady boyfriend was something new for me, but it was kind of fun being known as someone's girlfriend. Johnny was a great guy. We were always together anyway, so holding hands with Johnathon Benjamin Johnson just seemed normal to me.

Within a few weeks, Keith and Margaret decided to be girlfriend and boyfriend, so that made our group just that much closer. We went to church together, we talked on the phone every night, and we saw each other every day at school. Our lives couldn't get any better.

I still melted every time I got close to Andrew, but it was fun being a girlfriend to someone as well-liked as Johnny. Andrew went places with all of us as a group, but he never sat by any of the girls. We had a large group of friends and he just hung out with the other guys.

Only once did I see him sitting next to Carolyn, and for one second, I was overwhelmed with jealousy, but I instantly thought to myself, "He doesn't really belong to you, you just pretend he does. Besides you have a boyfriend, so get over it." That was the only time I ever saw him sitting next to any of the girls.

In November, Keith and I were going to take a week off from school and fly to Texas with our parents for our grandparent's 50th wedding anniversary. We were both A students, and we got our school work from our teachers in advance, so we wouldn't get behind while we were away.

Monday morning we got up early and boarded the plane for our trip to Texas. We were anxious to see all our relatives, because we had not seen many of them in several years. This would be like one big huge family reunion, with all our aunts, uncles, cousins, and shirt-tail relatives.

We stayed at a nice hotel a few miles from my grandparent's house. About 60 other family members also stayed at the same hotel. It was a large hotel and it was probably one of the nicest in the Dallas-Fort Worth area.

Our grandparent's fiftieth anniversary party was planned for Saturday, and they had invited a lot of people from all around the country. People were coming from everywhere; they even had some friends that were coming in from Spain. I was told that the man from Spain was an old army buddy of my grandpas.

My grandparents were very prominent in the Dallas area. My grandfather was a retired General, and after he retired from the military, he became the mayor of Dallas. So, they were very well known.

The party was to be held in the Crystal Ballroom at the hotel where we were staying. It was an exquisite room and we were told that it could hold a lot of people. My mother said there might be up to three or four hundred people at their anniversary party.

My family was very involved in politics, and the morning before the anniversary party many of us went down to the Crystal Ball room in our hotel to hear President John F. Kennedy speak. John F. Kennedy was the 35th President of the United States. Our teachers knew we would be attending this event, and they said it would be a once in a lifetime event so, they wanted Keith and I to write an extra-credit report about the President's speech, and tell our class about it when we got home. Thousands of people had gathered to catch a glimpse of Americas most popular political figure.

Our family listened to the President's inspiring speech, and after the speech was finished, we quickly walked down the street so that we could watch as the motorcade drove by with the President and his wife. Although, it had been raining earlier that morning, the sun was now out, and the rain had stopped. Luckily for us the motorcade was held up for a few moments while the first lady received a large bouquet of red roses. She took the large bouquet of roses with her when she climbed into the waiting limousine.

Governor John Connelly and his wife, Nellie were already seated in the front seat of the open convertible. The sun had come out, so they had taken off the plastic bubble top so that people could see the President and his wife more clearly. Vice President and Mrs. Johnson occupied another car that traveled behind the President and Mrs. Kennedy.

Our family cut through to the next street and rapidly walked a few blocks to find a place along the parade route that was a little closer to Dealey Plaza where the President's motorcade was headed. The motorcade slowly wound around and traveled through downtown Dallas on their way to the Trade Mart where the President planned to speak again. We found a great spot over near the Texas School Book Depository. There was plenty of room for all of us to stand together.

We soon observed the President's motorcade as it turned off Main Street and came down the street where our group was standing. We had a perfect place to see the smiling faces of the President and his wife, and to get some great pictures.

My dad flashed several pictures as President Kennedy looked directly at our group and waved, but as the President turned to wave to the people on the other side of the street, we heard gunfire coming from the tall building behind us. Every one of the people along that part of the parade route instantly fell to the ground as soon as we heard the bullets flying.

Suddenly, we realized that the President of the United States, President John F. Kennedy had been hit in the neck and head and was now slumped over towards Mrs. Kennedy and was no longer moving. Everyone up and down the street started screaming and crying. Even the small children covered their faces and sat down on the sidewalk and sobbed. We were all in shock. What was meant to be a very momentous occasion for everyone at the parade, ended up being one the most tragic events in American history.

Governor John Connally was also shot in the back. Hastily the convertible sped off to Parkland Memorial Hospital where President John F. Kennedy was given his last rites, and at 1:00 P.M. on Friday November 22, 1963, he was pronounced dead. He was only 46 years old.

A short time later, the President's body was placed in Air Force One where a grim-faced Lyndon B. Johnson took the oath of office. By 2:38 P.M., Lyndon B. Johnson became President of the United States.

A patrolman by the name of J. D. Tippits spotted the shooter carrying a rifle, but the shooter fatally shot Tippits before he could arrest him. Two days later, Lee Harvey Oswald was apprehended for the murder of President John F. Kennedy. They soon learned that Oswald shot the President with a rifle that he had purchase through the mail.

It was discovered that Oswald had been an employee at the Texas School Book Depository. It was from that location that he shot the President from a sixth-floor window. Our family members were standing watching the President's motorcade right in front of that building. We were only about fifteen feet away from the President's car when the shots began.

On Saturday the day after the shooting of the President, the Crystal Ballroom allowed my grandparents to go ahead and hold their fiftieth wedding anniversary as scheduled. It was a much more solemn event than originally planned, but hundreds of people came to show their admiration for my grandparents, and the celebration of fifty years of marriage.

At 12:30 P.M. on Sunday, November 24th, Oswald was scheduled to be transferred from police headquarters to the county jail. Viewers across America watched on live television coverage when a man suddenly appeared in the basement of the Dallas Police station carrying a pistol, and fired at point blank range and killed Lee Harvey Oswald. It was discovered that the assailant was a man by the name of Jack Ruby. Ruby, a local night club owner stated that he killed Oswald because he felt so bad for Mrs. Kennedy.

President John F. Kennedy's flag-draped casket was moved from the White House to the Capitol on a caisson drawn by six grey horses, accompanied by one riderless black horse. At the request of Mrs. Kennedy, the ceremonial details were modeled after the funeral of Abraham Lincoln.

Crowds that lined the street on Pennsylvania Avenue, mourned openly. For 21 hours the President's body lay in state in the Capitol Rotunda. 250,000 people filed by to pay their respects.

On Monday, November 25, 1963, President John F. Kennedy was laid to rest in the Arlington National Cemetery in Arlington, Virginia, directly across the Potomac River from Washington D.C. The funeral was attended by heads of state and representatives from more than 100 countries, with millions watching on television.

At the graveside, Mrs. Kennedy and her husband's brothers, Robert and Edward lit an eternal flame; and the entire Nation wept as three-year-old, John Kennedy Jr. saluted his father's casket, for one final goodbye.

On Tuesday morning, our family flew back home to Arlington, Massachusetts. I am sure that every person who witnessed the tragic killing of President John F. Kennedy would never be the same again. We knew the entire nation would be in total shock, and in mourning for countless days to come.

When Keith and I returned to school the following day, we were instantly met by students and teachers alike. All of them were rapidly asking questions and crying. The death of this President touched every single American, and the whole community knew that our family had witnessed the shooting first hand.

Before we even said anything, the entire student body, the school Principal, and all the teachers, had gathered around us in the middle of the school yard. Our school flag hung at half-staff in the center of the group. Each one of us closed our eyes in silent prayer for a few seconds, and for about twenty minutes we held on to each other and wept over the death of the President of the United States, John F. Kennedy.

When we went to our classes that day, every student was encouraged to talk about the events of the past few days. Some ask us questions, some just talked. We discussed the things we remembered about this President. One of the main things our age group remembered was that a few years earlier, President Kennedy had encouraged all Americans to build some sort of bomb shelter to protect their families from fallout in the event of a nuclear war with the Soviet Union, and to store plenty of canned goods. Most large buildings had bomb shelter signs directing people where to go in the event of an attack. It was a very fearful time for Americans.

Our teacher reminded us about the term, Duck and Cover that was introduced in 1951. She said it quickly became a part of the Civil Defense drills that every U.S. Citizen from children to the elderly, was encouraged to practice. They were to always be watchful and ready in the event of a nuclear attack. The Civil Defense plan was to hide under something and cover your face and head as a way of protecting yourself from a nuclear explosion.

Many cities had loud air raid sirens that went off at noon once a week, just for practice. If you were at school, you were instructed to hide under your desk and cover your head with your hands. The schools practiced Duck and Cover drills up until 1962, the year before President Kennedy was killed.

Between witnessing the death of the President of the United States, and then listening to all the comments about how unsafe our country now was, I was overcome with anxiety. My mind was on overload; I felt like it was the end of the world, and there was no one that could protect us. I was only 14 years old, with my whole life in front of me, but all I wanted to do was hide my face in my hands and cry.

When the class got their books out to study, I asked the teacher if I could be excused to be alone for a few minutes. I quickly walked out into the hall, and leaned up against the wall and covered my face and wept.

I was so upset I didn't even realize that someone was standing next to me. Then I felt his comforting arms gently wrap around me and pull me close, and I sobbed into his shoulder and chest. When I came to my senses, I looked up to see Andrew tenderly looking directly into my eyes.

We hugged for several minutes and then I gave him a slight smile and said, "Thank you, I guess I'd better get back to class." As I walked away, I thought to myself, "He truly is my courageous warrior."

Three

Homecoming

I went with Johnny for almost two years. He was such a sweetheart. It was fun having someone to go to the movies with and to all the school and church parties. Johnny was in most of my ninth-grade classes, and of course, we always ate lunch together each day along with a large group of friends. We very seldom ever went anywhere just the two of us. We usually had at least six or seven friends along wherever we went.

One night as my parents were watching the news on television, a **Special Report** came across the T.V. that said, "President Johnson has made the decision to send U.S. combat forces into battle in Vietnam." This report really upset my dad and mom, because it meant the United States would be going into war. Luckily, Keith was too young, but my parents had several friends who had young men who were older and just the right age.

The Vietnam War had been going on for several years, and President Johnson felt it was time for the United States to get more involved in the attempt to prevent the spread of communism. Of course, foreign policy, economic interest, natural fears, and geopolitical strategies also played a major role.

On April 7, 1965, President Johnson gave a speech at the John Hopkins University stating several reasons for escalating the U.S. involvement in Vietnam. After he secured Congressional Authorization with the Tonkin Gulf Resolution, Johnson launched a bombing campaign in the North, and by March he deployed 35,999 Marines to South Vietnam. He said our presence was there to help strengthen World Order. Within a few months several of the young men from our church were among those sent to be soldiers in Vietnam.

By the end of our ninth-grade school year, Johnny and his family had to move to Mississippi for a few months because his grandparents were getting older and they needed some help. Johnny's parents were both school teachers and they were off for the summer, so they just locked up their house and left it empty with plans to return in few months. Johnny told me, "I'll be back by the time school starts, and I promise to write every week while I am gone."

He was very good about writing, in fact sometimes he wrote twice a week. Every time I got a letter, I would write him right back. I could tell he was very anxious to leave

Mississippi. I was sure he was counting the days until he could be back home with his friends in Arlington, Massachusetts.

One day he sadly wrote that there was a lot of racial tension taking place in Mississippi and his family decided they needed to stay with the grandparents for a little while longer. He told me that in August, three months before John F. Kennedy was killed, Martin Luther King Jr. had given a famous speech called 'I have a Dream', at the Lincoln Memorial in Washington DC. Over 200,000 people gathered to hear him speak. It was at that time that Mississippi was chosen as the site of the Freedom Summer Project due to its historically low levels of African American voters.

Johnny's older sister was one of about 700 white volunteers that was working on a Mississippi summer project, called Freedom Summer. It was a voter registration drive aimed at increasing the number of registered Black voters in Mississippi.

Around that time, Johnny's letters started changing. He told me that he was scared all the time, and he hated being in Mississippi. He said he never left his grandparent's house. He said he just stayed home all day, because he was afraid to go anywhere.

A short time later, we saw on television that there were murders, bombings, and kidnappings very near the area where Johnny's grandparents lived. They said the Freedom Summer volunteers were met with violent resistance from the Ku Klux Klan. I feared for Johnny's family, but I also understood why they were afraid to leave his grandparents there all alone with so much violence all around them.

I prayed for him every day, and I especially missed him when school started. He had been one of my best friends since we were in grade school, and it was really different not having him around on the first day of school. Johnny wrote me that his parents had enrolled him in a small private Christian school near his grandparent's house. He said his parents were not going back to teaching for a while at least for the next few months.

It was our sophomore year and Keith and I had chosen to be in a school jazz band. We both played the piano, but Keith also played the drums. I enjoyed playing the piano, and even as a teenager I was oftentimes the church organist during worship time.

The jazz band class was small, but I was glad to see my good friend Mark in the group. Mark played the saxophone. We had 5 saxophone players, 4 trumpet players, 3 trombone players, and a clarinet player. Keith was on the drums, and then there was my 'courageous warrior' Andrew on the electric guitar. Yes, Andrew was in my jazz band class, so of course that became my favorite class period.

School had been going for about 5 weeks and our band was getting really good. We were lucky because every one of us had been playing our instruments for a long time, and so it was easier for us to blend together. Jazz band was fun because it was so fast and bouncy.

One Friday afternoon Andrew asked me if I could stay after class with him for a few minutes to go over a couple of songs together. Our group was going to perform at an assembly in two weeks and he wanted to practice alone with me.

He sat down beside me on the piano bench and we placed the music on the music rack, of the piano. We played two songs, and when we finished, he looked at me and innocently asked, "Are you still going with Johnny Johnson? I haven't seen him around school this year."

As he talked, he never stopped staring directly into my face. He was only about ten inches away from me as he sincerely asked about Johnny. I was caught off-guard as I stared into his gorgeous deep-blue eyes. He was so handsome; I think he was even more handsome than the first time that I saw him. I was not sure what to say, because although I wrote to Johnny all the time, I had not actually seen him for over four months, and I was not sure when I would see him again.

I timidly replied as I looked down at my hands, and then back at Andrew, "Johnny and I have been good friends for many years, but he has been staying in Mississippi with his family for several months."

Andrew bashfully smiled, still looking directly into my face, and said, "Well, do you think maybe I could take you to the Homecoming dance?"

I felt like leaping up and down, I couldn't believe it. I had waited for over three years for Andrew. So, I calmly replied, "That would nice, I would love to go with you." As my brain was screaming inside my head...YES, YES, YES!

He grinned and said, "Great, I was almost afraid to ask you, but I wanted to ask before some of the other guys did."

He slowly collected the music off the piano and said, "Thank you for practicing these songs. Can I walk you out?"

"Sure," I calmly answered. While thinking inside my head, "I am going to Homecoming with Andrew Paul Brookshire the 3rd, my manly, brave, strong, courageous warrior. The most handsome guy in the school." I felt like skipping, but I just collected my music and walked out gracefully.

The very next day, my mom and I went shopping for a dress. I was so excited I couldn't stop smiling. Andrew was the sweetest, cutest, smartest, most polite guy I had ever been around, and he was nice to his grandma. He was strong, tall, confident and he looked like movie star. I was so ecstatic I felt like I was a princess and my prince was taking me to the Homecoming dance.

Going to Homecoming was new to me. I had never gone before, so I didn't know what kind of dress to buy. I finally decided on a deep blue chiffon V-neck beaded dress, with long beaded see-through sleeves. I wore matching blue shoes, and as I twirled around in front of the store mirror, I once again felt like royalty.

Each day after that, Andrew and I would talk and sometimes he would even walk me down the hall. A few days before the Homecoming dance, he asked for my phone number so he could call me and make plans for our date. "Our date; this was going to be a real date," I thought to myself. Johnny and I always went places together, but with a large group, but I was going on a date with Andrew all alone.

The night before the dance Andrew called me on the phone and we talked for over an hour. We talked longer than we had ever talked before. He said he would pick me up in his dad's car around 6:00 the next day.

Promptly at 6:00 the doorbell rang and my mom went to the door. I was all ready to go, and I slowly walked in from the kitchen area to greet my date.

Andrew looked amazing in his dark suite, white shirt, and dark blue tie. He smiled from ear to ear when he saw me walk in the room. He carried a beautiful white corsage, that my mom helped pin onto my dress. My mom and dad took several pictures of us and then the two of us headed out the door.

Andrew politely opened the passenger side car door for me, and then he went around to the driver's side to get in. Everything seemed unreal. It was so perfect. We stopped at a small restaurant where several of our friends from church, were meeting us for dinner before the dance.

About an hour later, we walked into the beautifully decorated school auditorium. It was exquisite, with banners, balloons, and colorful decorations. There was a man at the entrance, that took each couple's picture as they walked through the door. We heard fun, bouncy music playing as we walked in.

Several of our friends were already dancing, "Do you want to dance?" Andrew asked me. I nodded my head up and down and smiled as Andrew led me out to the dance floor. It was a fast song called 'I only want to be with you.' I loved to dance, and to my surprising delight, Andrew was a great dancer. After the song was over, we walked over to the side of the room and stood by the wall.

"Where did you learn to dance like that?" I asked Andrew.

"My mother taught me to dance when I was only a few years old," he answered timidly.

The next song started and this time it was a slow dance called 'Unchained Melody.' We just smiled at each other, and walked out onto the dance floor. When he took me in his arms, it just seemed right. Johnny had hugged me before, but it wasn't the same. As Andrew and I continued to dance, he gently pulled me closer and closer until I put my face up next to the bottom of his cheek, and I knew he was the love of my life.

We danced a few more dances and then we walked out on the walkway with several other friends. Everyone was laughing and joking. Many were hugging each other or holding hands as we innocently stood around and talked. The air was turning chilly and the girls were starting to complain, but still no one moved or went inside.

Suddenly, I felt Andrew put his coat around my shoulders, and he left his arm in place and drew me closer to his side to keep me warm. As I turned and saw his handsome face just inches away from mine, I spontaneously cuddled my head against his neck as he pulled me tighter and tighter in his arms. Everything we did just seemed natural, as if it was the way it was supposed to be.

Towards the end of the evening, they called our names to come up on stage along with two other couples and we were named 'Best-looking couple' of the sophomore class. They also had a couple from the Junior class, and a couple from the Senior class.

We danced, we talked, and we laughed with friends. The Homecoming dance was probably one of the most enchanting nights of my life. I had just turned sixteen years old a few weeks earlier, and tonight I was dancing with the prince-charming of my dreams.

Everything had gone so perfect; I did not want the night to end. I feared by morning my wonderful fairytale would disappear. As Andrew walked me to my door after the dance, I turned and looked into his gorgeous eyes, and before he could say anything I gently put my hands on the sides of his face, and tenderly kissed him goodnight.

After he left, my mom and I stayed up until 2:00 in the morning talking about the perfect evening that I had with my brave, strong, courageous warrior, Andrew Paul Brookshire the 3rd. That night, when I finally fell asleep, I once again dreamed that I could see Andrew and I standing up in front of a church, and we were getting married. My dream looked different somehow, but I could not quite tell why it was different.

From that night on, everyone knew that we were a couple. Everyone except for Johnny. Johnny still wrote to me regularly, but his letters had started getting more distant. His grandmother had gotten worse and his family planned to stay in Mississippi until the end of the school year. Johnny said he would finish his sophomore class in Mississippi then the family would be home by summer. I let him know that I had gone to Homecoming with Andrew, and to my surprise he gave us his blessing. Johnny was such a good friend to me, and I knew he always would be.

Our band teacher asked Andrew and I if we would do a song together for the next school assembly. Andrew often performed at school assemblies, and I played the piano and sang a lot at church, but we had never really sung and played together, until then. We decided to do an old song that had recently been made popular by Elvis Pressley called, 'How Great Thou Art.' Apparently, people liked us singing that song because we ended up performing it several other times for church and other youth events.

Once we did our first duet together, we were asked to sing at every assembly, and often at church. Andrew and I were so much alike. We had the same religious beliefs, we were both very positive people, we liked the same music, the same kind of food, and the same movies. We were always together. I never told anyone about my dreams, but we both knew that everything about our relationship was right. We sang together, we went to the same church, we had the same friends, and we could never imagine our lives without each other.

When his grandmother passed away, my entire family went to her funeral. Andrew told me that his grandmother had been a strong influence on him. He said, "My grandmother's parents were missionaries, and my grandmother had been born in Africa, and she had lived an extraordinary life." He stated, "I learned so much from her. She is the reason I want to be in the ministry."

I hugged him and smiled, but I never told him the spiritual impact his grandmother also had on me the first time I saw her in church, when I was only thirteen years old.

By our senior year, we had been inseparable for so long that our moms and dads had also become very good friends. He loved my parents, and I loved his parents. Our families did a lot of things together, and we knew that we would always be family.

I thanked the Lord every day for the many blessings that he gave us. Andrew was kind, handsome, mature, thoughtful, intelligent, and polite. We both felt older than we actually were. When other friends our age were out partying and getting in trouble, we were at home having dinner with our families and planning for our future.

My Andrew was perfect in every way. We both knew that God had put us together for a reason, and our lives could not be happier. Every day we talked about our future. We looked forward to graduating, and having a big church wedding. We both wanted to have four children, and live in Arlington. Andrew planned to be a minister, and I planned to be a minister's wife. I loved Andrew so much, and I knew that he loved me.

Four

1 Thessalonians 5:16-18

During our senior year the war in Vietnam grew deadlier and deadlier. In fact, 1968 was the deadliest year of the war for the United States, 246 Americans were killed in one day. More and more young men were being drafted every month. Many of the guys in our town were being drafted shortly after graduating from high school.

In February, Andrew went to register for the draft, along with my brother Keith, Johnny, Mark, and several other friends in our class. Suddenly, the war that had always been on the other side of the world, was now coming to Arlington, Massachusetts. For the first time in my life, I was overcome with constant anxiety and fear.

My brother Keith was rejected from the draft because of problems that he had when we were born. Twins often have problems during delivery, partly because they usually have a low birth-weight, and they are crowded because the mother is carrying two babies. Keith and I were both born very small, and he had to have several surgeries the first year after we were born. Of course, Andrew, Mark, and Johnny passed all the tests with flying colors, so they were put on a list until their numbers came up.

One of the most popular songs around that time was 'The Ballad of the green Berets.' Andrew sang that song in a school assembly; and he did a fantastic job, but I just sat and cried though the entire song, because it was a song of the war about fearless men who jump and die.

I was numb inside. It was inevitable that any day Andrew's number would be called for the draft. Within just a few short months, the Vietnam War had become very personal to me. My Andrew would soon be going to war, and I didn't know how I could bear it. I tried not to think about it, but I knew our perfect world would soon be coming to an end.

In May, many of us helped decorate for our senior prom. The school rented a large hall at a nice hotel, and we worked for two days to make the room picture-perfect. My mom and I once again found a wonderful dress for the occasion, but my mind was constantly in a state of dread and sadness. I was smiling on the outside, but my heart was breaking on the inside.

At the prom, I was voted Prom Queen and Andrew was voted as the Prom King. It was such an incredible way to end our senior year. The prom was absolutely fantastic, and for one night we felt as if we didn't have a care in the world.

Eight days before graduation several of the guys from our class received notices that they were to report to the draft board in three weeks. Their numbers were being called, and they were to report for duty. Of course, my Andrew was on that list.

I was so distraught I felt sick. I was so sad that I could not even cry. Andrew was my life, and even as a teenager I knew he was my soulmate; he was my everything. I sometimes had to tell myself to think because I couldn't believe this was happening to my ideal world.

I walked around for the last few days of school in a complete daze. My mind was confused, my heart was broken, and my flawless anticipated life was now in a whirlwind. All the plans that we had made for our future were disappearing before my eyes, and there was nothing that I could do to stop it. All I could do was take one step at a time, trying to make sense of everything that had happened.

Each evening I would pray myself to sleep, yet, within a few hours I would wake up crying in the middle of the night. I read my Bible verses over and over, I sang gospel songs, I tried everything to keep my mind off the fact that my perfect, talented Andrew was going off to war.

Andrew and I were still teenagers, we were just graduating from High School. This should have been the happiest time in our life; we were supposed to have our entire lives ahead of us, but instead I was terrified about the future.

Whenever Andrew was around, I held onto him, and I wouldn't let him go.

Andrew was so proper; he always did the right thing. He continually tried to encourage me that everything was going to be alright. He sincerely told me, "There is a war going on, and it is only right, that I step up, and do my part for America." He was so much braver than I was.

The night before Andrew was to leave, we went to the park and walked by the river. I couldn't stop crying, because everything seemed so unreal. I knew that by this time tomorrow I would be all alone, and Andrew, Mark and Johnny would be off on a plane and headed for war.

Andrew had me sit down on a bench beside him, and he said, "I have something for you." He had been carrying a bag all the time we were walking, and he held the package behind his back so that I couldn't see it until he was ready to give it to me.

He handed me the package and inside was a soft, cuddly teddy bear holding a big red embroidered heart that said 'MY FOREVER LOVE.' Andrew then looked directly into my eyes and he said, "I want you to hold this teddy bear and squeeze it tightly every time you are sad." Then he reached into his pocket and pulled out a small jewelry gift box, and handed me a beautiful gold chain with half a broken heart that also said, 'MY FOREVER LOVE.' I was crying so hard that I couldn't see. Andrew put the chain around my neck and whispered, "Wear this, and never take it off until we are together again."

The next day most of the town was there to send our young men off to war. As I kissed Andrew goodbye one last time, he handed me two letters in sealed envelopes; and then he was gone. He was headed for Boot camp at Fort Dix in New Jersey, and then overseas. I felt like screaming, I was so helpless. I just stood at the gate shaking and wailing on the inside. From now on I knew I had to be an adult; because my youth had boarded the plane along with Andrew, and flew off to war.

All the way home I just stared out the window of the car and didn't talk. I had the two envelopes in my lap, but I couldn't get myself to open them. I held the teddy bear in my left arm, and I tightly gripped my right hand around the beautiful gold broken-heart necklace that Andrew had given me. Everything was a blur, and I didn't know how I was going to survive until Andrew came back.

When we got home, I silently walked up to my room and closed the door behind me. I still didn't feel like reading the letters that Andrew had given me, so I placed them in the top drawer of my dresser, and walked over and sat in my window seat. I buried my face into the precious teddy bear, and squeezed it as hard as I could, but I couldn't stop crying. I did not move, I just sat there crying for hours. I had no concept of time, but I finally realized that it had gotten dark outside, and I was now staring into the darkness.

I covered my face with my hands and screamed, "Lord, help me, I am fearful of so many things, and I don't know how I can survive the next few months while Andrew is gone to war." I shook my head back and forth and whispered out loud, "War... Andrew is not just away for a few months; he is gone off to war!" I whimpered into the teddy bear and pleaded, "Lord, I am so afraid, because I know that so many young soldiers are dying every day, and I love Andrew so much, I just couldn't bear it if something happened to him."

As I sat alone in the dark room, I heard a light tapping at my door. My brother Keith opened the door, and came in and sat beside me in the darkness. He gently put his arm around my shoulder and pulled me close to him, and we sat together and cried. Keith knew how much I loved Andrew, but I suddenly realized that not only Andrew was gone, but most of Keith's best friends had just boarded a plane, and left Arlington to go off to war. And for the first time in Keith's life his friends were gone, and he was left behind.

We sat in the darkness holding each other for several minutes, until our mom came in carrying a tray with 3 bowls of hot clam chowder, Vermont common crackers, milk and a freshly made Boston crème pie. My wonderful mother took the tray out to the deck, that was in the front of my bedroom, and the three of us sat down at a small table and quietly ate. I had no idea what time it was. Because time no longer mattered, I had nothing to do but wait.

Late that night I tried to fall asleep, but my thoughts kept spinning around and around. About 3:00 in the morning I suddenly remembered the letters that Andrew had given me, and I got out of bed and walked over to the dresser, and took them out of the drawer.

This was the first time I had even tried to look at them. As I picked up the first letter, I saw it was written to me, but to my surprise the second letter was written to my father. So, I placed the letter for my father back into the drawer. I held onto to my letter for a few seconds almost afraid to read what was inside. Finally, I timidly tore open the envelope, and held the paper in my hand. The letter said:

To My Forever Love Kathryn,

Although our lives are now put on hold for a while, you will always be with me in my heart, no matter where I am throughout the world. If we are together or if we are thousands of miles apart; you will always be my forever love. Someday we will have that big church wedding, our four children, and a beautiful house in Arlington. I will be a minister and you will be a minister's wife. Thank you for bringing such joy to my life. I knew that you were the love of my life the very first time I saw you.

Say this memory verse every day, and visualize that I am there saying it beside you.

1 Thessalonians 5:16-18, Rejoice always, pray continually, give thanks in all circumstances; for this is God's will for you in Christ Jesus.

I will always love you,

Your forever love Andrew

The next day I handed the second envelope to my dad, but he just put it in a drawer and did not even look at it. So, I didn't know what it said.

Five

A Time of Change

I received mail from Andrew at least twice a week while he was in boot camp. His letters were very sweet and upbeat. He felt good about being in the military and preparing to fight for his country, but he knew that his unit would be shipping out soon, and he wouldn't be able to write as often.

In a few of his letters, he had mentioned a young black man from North Carolina that was only 14 years old. He said that this young boy named Dan Bullock, altered the date of his birth certificate so that he could join his friends and be a marine. Dan was raised in Goldsboro, North Carolina. Andrew told me that Dan really had a hard time in basic training because he was so young, so Andrew and several of the other guys, in his unit helped him get through. Three days after his fifteenth birthday Dan Bullock, headed overseas.

We saw on television that the war was getting more deadly every day. Each night I would close my eyes and repeat the memory verse that Andrew shared with me, but as the time got closer for his unit to go to Vietnam my faith grew weaker. The more frightened I became, the more often I repeated the memory verse each day. I knew it by heart, and I felt Andrew was with me each time I would close my eyes and repeat it.

Andrew sadly wrote me that a few weeks after his young friend, Dan Bullock left, they got word that he had been killed in a small-arms fight while he was on night watch, a short time after he arrived in Vietnam. The army then discovered that he had only recently turned 15 years old. It was then reported to the national news, that Dan Bullock of Goldsboro, North Carolina was the youngest soldier killed in Vietnam. The emotional letter that Andrew sent me about Dan's death was the last letter that I received.

After that, all letters stopped. No one heard from any of the young men that had left Arlington on the plane that day. We decided that they must have finished boot camp, and left the United States for Vietnam. I found myself praying continuously. I could hardly think about anything else, but my sweet, darling Andrew traveling clear across the world to a war-torn country. I talked to his mother every day, and she never heard from him either.

Some days I caught myself praying all day long. It was hard to concentrate on anything else. I spent each day just waiting, but weeks went by and no letters ever came. I got so I couldn't eat or sleep. I started losing weight, and my family became very concerned about me.

Then one afternoon, my dad came home from work, and told us that he had received word that his company needed a new Vice President of Marketing in a town called Boise, Idaho. He timidly told all of us that he felt he should take this position and we should move clear across the country to this peaceful little town called Boise.

I panicked, and refused to go. I had a terrible fear of Andrew writing to me, or coming home and not being able to find me if I was clear on the other side of the United States. I begged my parents to let me stay in Arlington, but within a few days Keith convinced me to go with them. He told me, "Please go with us, I do not want to go all the way across America by myself. We are twins, and we have always been together, and I am not ready to be separated now." He also sadly told me, "I have already lost most of my friends, and I don't want to lose you too."

Within a few weeks, the house was emptied, and we were packed up and ready to move 2,700 miles, all the way across America to an unfamiliar place called Idaho. Our parents told us it would take several weeks to get there. They wanted us to relax, and stop and see a few of the interesting places across America. Then my mother told us, "The last few months have been so stressful with graduation, and Andrew and the other boys leaving, that it will be good to get away and think about something else for a while."

I walked up to my room, and put my hands over my face and thought, "I don't want to think about something else. I just want my Andrew to be home, and for things to be like they were six months ago." I shook my head and prayed, "Oh Lord, I don't know if I can get through this." Then I recited out loud the memory verse, I shared with Andrew 1 Thessalonians 5:16-18, Rejoice always, pray continually, give thanks in all circumstances; for this is God's will for you in Christ Jesus.

The day we left, I called Andrew's mother Juliette, one last time, just to see if she had heard from him in the past few hours. Of course, she had not heard anything. Andrew's mother hadn't been well, that is why I faithfully checked on her every single day. She knew I would be leaving that morning, and I would not be able to call her every day like I had been doing.

His mother sadly said, "I was told that it was very common for families not to hear for several weeks, once the soldiers had been shipped out." She started to cry and she told me, "Kathryn, I am so sorry, I can't believe that just a short time ago you and Andrew were planning your lives, and you had everything worked out, and now he's gone, and we can't talk to him or even know where he is." His poor mother kept crying as she told me goodbye, and that she loved me. I was crying too, as I told her how much I loved Andrew's entire family. I promised to send her my new address just as soon as we got to Idaho. My heart was breaking as we pulled out of the driveway, and headed for our new life.

I was completely unaware of our surroundings as we traveled for the first hundred miles. Keith seemed almost excited about the move, but of course I wasn't. He watched out the window and commented about the beautiful fields, and the many different colored cows. I sat in the back seat of the car hugging my teddy bear, and trying to calm down, but my heart was shattering, and my mind was screaming inside my head. My mother was very concerned about me so she gave me a light sleeping pill that she had gotten for me from our family doctor the day before we left.

Eventually, I fell into a deep sleep and slept for hours. Right before I woke up, I once again had the dream about Andrew and me getting married. This time the dream was a little different. Andrew looked different, and no matter how hard I tried, I couldn't quite tell what was different about him. I was facing Andrew, and I could only see the back of my head, but I was sure it was me standing with Andrew.

I had to admit, I did feel better after getting some rest. It was almost time to stop at the hotel for the night, and then have some dinner. For the first time in several weeks, I almost felt hungry. We pulled into a beautiful hotel somewhere near the highway, where my dad had made reservations. We checked into our room, and then headed for dinner down in the hotel restaurant.

After dinner, Keith and I went swimming in the hotel pool. Soon my mom and dad came down to the pool area, and got into the hot tub that was next to the pool. Eventually, Keith and I joined them in the nice, warm hot tub. It was so relaxing, it felt wonderful.

We went back to our room and went to bed. I fell asleep shortly after saying my memory verse and my prayers. It was probably the first time I had fallen asleep so easily since Andrew left, and for some reason, I slept all night long. The next morning, we got up early, because we had a long day of traveling. I woke up feeling much better than I had in weeks. We ate a good breakfast down in the hotel restaurant and then headed for New York. We planned to go see Niagara Falls; it is about a twenty-minute drive from Buffalo, New York.

We checked into an exquisite hotel near the falls around 4:00 in the afternoon. The hotel was called the Sheraton Falls View Hotel. It was one of the most magnificent hotels I had ever seen. We had a view of the falls right out of our hotel room window. In fact, there were windows everywhere and in one direction we could see the falls, and the other direction we could see a giant antique Ferris wheel with colorful stores, restaurants, and the huge casino along the endless sidewalks.

My mom told us, “This is one of my favorite places on earth. We plan to stay here for several days, because there is so much to see, and we want you to see it all.”

The Niagara Falls State Park is New York’s oldest State Park, it opened in 1885. The Park covers over 400 acres that include nature and hiking trails and picnic facilities. 4-6 million cubic feet of water rush over the falls, every minute of the day.

The thundering roars and shimmering rainbows of Niagara Falls consists of three waterfalls on the Niagara River. It is on the border between New York and Ontario, Canada. The Observation Tower at Prospect Point extends out over the Niagara Falls Gorge Discovery Center viewpoints. It also leads to other center viewpoints along the way. The falls at Niagara Falls are among the most impressive and best-known falls in the world. Masses of water from Lake Erie plunge over almost a 200-foot drop to flow into Ontario.

We had a late dinner down in the hotel restaurant. The elegant restaurant had floor to ceiling windows looking out onto the colorful lit-up falls. There were multiple-colored lights pointed from every angle towards the massive water falls. Niagara Falls is beautiful in the daytime, but it is absolutely breathtaking after the sun goes down. We felt like royalty as we sat in the picture-perfect hotel restaurant and ate our magnificent meal, and watched the spectacular water falls. Our parents told us that this is where they had spent their honeymoon twenty -two years ago. They loved Niagara Falls and that is why they wanted to share it with us.

That night as I went to bed, I repeated my memory verse and said my prayers, and thought about Andrew. As I prayed for Andrew, I wished he could be here with me to share this beautiful hotel, and the wonders of Niagara

Falls. As I drifted off to sleep, I silently whispered, "Goodnight, Andrew. I love you and miss you more than you could ever know."

The next day we ate lunch at the Top of the Falls Restaurant before leaving for the 'Maid of the Mist' boat excursion. Later we explored the area around the Cave of the Winds 175 feet into the Niagara Gorge, and we experienced the power of the falls from the Hurricane Deck. Niagara Falls was a magnificent experience. We could see why this was our mother's favorite place on earth.

On Thursday morning, we woke up bright and early after four glorious days in paradise, and sadly said goodbye to our wonderful hotel room, and the incredible beauty of Niagara Falls. Today we would head to Hershey, Pennsylvania a town full of rich history and fun.

Our parents had made reservations at an old hotel called the Hotel Hershey. The hotel is a historic landmark and a five-star hotel. The Fountain Lobby Hotel Hershey opened on May 26, 1933 during the depression.

The stately hotel sits atop Pat's Hill over-looking Milton S. Hershey's Chocolate factory in Hershey, Pennsylvania. It has 276 guest rooms and a 23,5000 square foot event center. Hershey and his wife had traveled abroad many times and they wanted the hotel to have a Spanish patio, with tiled floors, a fountain, and a circular dining room with a view from every table. The hotel had been a dream of Milton Hershey and his wife, Catherine for many years. Yet,

Catherine died several years before the grand hotel was completed.

The Hershey chocolate factory was constructed nearly three decades earlier, before they decided to build the hotel. Building the hotel during the depression was very hard, but Hershey decided that he could better serve the towns construction workers by paying them to build the hotel rather than providing for their welfare if no one was working. The town had over 600 construction workers.

At the opening of the hotel, Milton Hershey had a big dinner-dance with over 400 invited guests to celebrate the completion of the hotel. He patterned the giant hotel after hotels that he and Catherine had stayed in on the Mediterranean.

The Hershey Hotel is characterized by great luxury of detail and elegance with tinted walls, palms, and fountains. It is adorned in colored and grilled woodworks and brilliant hangings and rugs. A botanical display garden is just south of the Hotel with more than 20 acres of beautiful roses arranged in formal beds. There are over 7,000 different displays of colorful roses. The Hotel Hershey is recognized as one of the greatest resorts in North America.

At the same time Hershey built the magnificent hotel, he also built a community building and a junior-senior high school on Pat's Hill as a school for boys who had lost one or both of their parents.

The Hershey Trolley Works sightseeing tour tells the story of Milton S. Hershey, and you also visit the original chocolate factory, and the Milton Hershey School and the original farm home. One of the highlights of the Hershey Chocolate Factory is that kids can make their own personal chocolate Hershey bar.

The Hershey Amusement Park is rated the best amusement park in the northwest by Family Magazine. It has rides, the boardwalk, the water park, and the entertainment show. Zoo America has a walk-through zoo, and the zoo is right next-door to Hershey Park. The zoo has more than 200 animals from the North American region.

Before we checked out of the hotel, my mother let me call Andrew's mother on the hotel telephone. Her phone rang quite a few times, but no one answered. I called her number several times before we left, but I never talked to anyone. I guess she wasn't home.

The historic hotel had incredible food, so before we got in the car to head for Ohio, we had breakfast at the Hershey Grill located at the Hershey Lodge Resort. Keith and I both had their specialty, S'mores French Toast, it was amazing.

After breakfast, we were on the road again; this time we were headed for The Rock and Roll Hall of Fame on the shores of Lake Erie in Cleveland, Ohio. We spent one day at the Rock and Roll Museum, and on our second day in Cleveland we visited the Cleveland Art Museum. It is the fourth wealthiest art museum in the United States, admission is free, because it is supported by massive endowment funds. Both museums were wonderful.

That night before we went to bed, I once again tried to call Andrew's mother, but still no one answered. I felt very concerned, but then I thought maybe she was finally getting out of the house more. When we were still living in Arlington, she never went anywhere; she continually just waited to hear from Andrew, so perhaps not being able to reach her was good news. My parents told me I could try again as soon as we reached the next hotel.

I had to admit, this trip was really helping me to calm down, because I began feeling better every day. Of course, I continually thought and prayed for Andrew and his family, but I did not feel overcome with the heavy fear and depression that I had in Arlington. Seeing so many wonderful places on the trip, had really inspired me to think about other things. Keith was thoroughly enjoying himself too, he laughed and talked and joked just like he normally did. My mother was right, this change of scenery was helping every one of us.

Our next stop would be Kentucky, and I would once again try to reach Andrew's parents. We were headed for the Mammoth Cave National Park. It is the home to thousands of years of human history and rich diversity of plant and animal life. It has the world's longest known cave system, and Mammoth Cave National Park is the World Heritage Set and International Biosphere Reserve.

Before leaving Kentucky, I once again, called Andrew's parents, but no one answered. I wasn't sure what to think, but I knew all I could do was continue to call until I finally reached someone.

Over the next two weeks we traveled through Illinois, Iowa and on to the breathtaking Black Hills of South Dakota. Our family then headed to Wyoming to the spectacular Yellowstone National Park. After seeing the deep clear pools and geysers and hiking the boardwalks throughout the park, we headed off for the last leg of our fantastic adventure down to Zion National Park in Utah.

All the magnificent arches throughout the Utah dessert were unlike anything any of us had ever seen before. We took a guided sightseeing bus tour through Zion Canyon Scenic Drive, and stopped at many unbelievable locations. The jagged cliffs and steep stone arches were some of God's finest creations. Visiting the canyons was truly an extraordinary ending to our incredible journey across America. My parents were right, this trip was a definite blessing to our entire family.

We had been gone from Arlington, Massachusetts for almost four weeks by the time we got to Idaho. I still had not been able to reach anyone at Andrew's house. My mother finally called one of our old neighbors in Arlington, Mrs. Jane Shepherd to see if she knew anything about Andrew or his parents. Mrs. Shepherd said that she hadn't heard anything about his family, but she wrote down our new Idaho phone number, and promised to call us if she found out anything.

Six

Idaho

The new house in Boise was amazing. It was much like our home in Arlington with its massive wrap around porch, high ceilings and antique restored bannisters, fireplaces, and wood-workings. Our surprising new residence was set back on the property with a huge lush green lawn and numerous manicured trees and hedges, just like our property in Massachusetts.

The year that we moved to Boise, Idaho, there were approximately 70,000 people that lived in the area. When we left Massachusetts the population of Arlington, was approximately 53, 000. Both cities were very similar in size and population, yet, Boise was the capital of Idaho.

Our family's new home was located on Harrison Boulevard, in an established area where most of the houses were built more than 100 years earlier. Harrison Boulevard is part of the city's, oldest living history. It is a place where you might sit and have a cup of hot tea in the very room that was once used by governors or other dignitaries, or you might cook dinner in a kitchen used by one of Idaho's many millionaires. At one time, Harrison Boulevard had tracks used as Boise's electric trolley car system.

The charming boulevard was a divided tree-lined street in the North End with homes built between 1901 to 1942. The beautiful Boulevard was originally named 17th Street, but it was renamed in honor of President Benjamin Harrison, who signed the act that gave Idaho statehood in 1891.

In 1910 developers planted 3,000 Elm and Maple trees throughout the neighborhood. Over the years Harrison Boulevard has been home to numerous well-known people like: J. R. Simplot, Harry Morrison, many supreme court justices, numerous politicians, three Boise Mayors and two Governors. In later years, the street and the adjacent area was listed in the National Register of Historic Places, by 1989, it also became a Boise historic district.

From the very beginning, our new house felt like home. Within a few days, our father started his new position as Vice President of Marketing, in his Idaho office. Our house was only about a mile away from our dad's office building. His office was in a tall building, right in the center of town, in downtown Boise. Unlike driving in to Boston every day from Arlington, he could almost walk to work when the weather was good.

My mom, Keith, and I worked diligently putting our new house together. We shopped, we planned and we decorated. Our new home was magnificent. I decorated my bedroom in deep greens and clean, fluffy whites. Once again, my room was my very favorite room in the entire enormous house. Although we had enjoyed our fantastic trip across America, we were all glad to get our new house organized and put everything in its place.

The people of Idaho were very friendly. Even the neighbors along our beautiful Harrison boulevard soon welcomed us, and made us feel like we belonged. I thought of Andrew continually, I placed my Andrew bear in the center of my bed, and hugged it several times each day. I continually wore the broken heart necklace around my neck, and I had never taken it off since the night Andrew put it on me. Everything I did included Andrew in my plans; I could hardly wait to show him our new house in Idaho.

I called Andrew's mother every day, but no one ever answered. Six weeks after we got settled into our house, our old neighbor Mrs. Shepherd called and said she still had never talked to Andrew's parents. She even stopped by their house three times, but no one was ever home. She said she promised to call if she did ever hear anything.

I too continued to call every day, the phone would ring, but no one answered. I constantly repeated my memory verse and prayed for Andrew; he was always on my mind. Yet, I realized that moving to Idaho was a good change for me, because I didn't have the overpowering dread that I continually had back in Arlington. My mind was much more positive, and I slept and ate better.

We started to attend a church with a family of one of the men that worked with my dad. It was very different for me at first, because the church where I met Andrew was the only church that I had ever gone to.

There was a large college-age group and Keith fit in instantly. Within a few weeks Keith had a new girlfriend, so he couldn't have been happier, and he acted like he had lived in Idaho all his life.

Several of the young men in our group asked me out, but I told them I was waiting for Andrew to come home from Vietnam, and we planned to be married. I became friends with a lot of the guys and I went to every outing, but I never accepted a date from any of them. I always went alone.

Almost every person I talked to knew someone who had been drafted and was overseas, many of them had lost their fathers, their brothers, their uncles, or a neighbor. As much as I loved Andrew, it was kind of embarrassing for me that I was so devoted to him, yet I never heard from Andrew or his family. I felt almost like I was making it up that I was going to marry Andrew, and he wasn't even real.

So many changes had taken place in my life over the past several months, and lately they had all become good changes. Our family enjoyed living in Idaho, my dad liked his job, we loved our wonderful new house, and we were even getting used to our new church. Coming to Idaho was a wise move for my parents to make, it was a huge adjustment for all of us, but the timing couldn't be better.

I was slowly beginning to realize that my parents had come to Idaho for Keith and me. They wanted to get us as far away from Arlington as they could, because we just had too much heartache after graduation. I had been so depressed every day, and I was absolutely obsessed about Andrew leaving, and Keith and I were forced to say goodbye to so many of our good friends who had gone off to war; it was just unbearable.

Our whole life in Arlington had transformed. We needed a completely new start, and that is exactly what Idaho offered us. My dad didn't want me to fret about being so far away, so he promised to fly me back to Arlington just as soon we got word that Andrew was home from Vietnam. From there we could decide what we wanted to do, and where we wanted to live. So, even living 2,700 miles from Massachusetts, didn't discourage me, because I knew that once I got word from Andrew, I could just fly back to be with him.

Days passed and I called Arlington every day, but I still had never reached anyone. We contacted several people from our old church, but no one had seen Andrew's parents. Keith and I had both started classes at the local college. I repeated my memory verse every night after saying my prayers, but I could not help but be worried and confused after not hearing anything for so long. I tried to keep a positive attitude, but I knew in my heart something was wrong.

One day Mrs. Shepherd called and ask us for our address in Idaho. She said she wanted our address in case she heard from Andrew or his parents. My mother gave it to her, and then once again we waited.

It had been months since I had received Andrew's last letter, and that was when he was still in boot camp. I understood that a lot of people didn't get much mail from their family members who were in the service, but I was beginning to feel completely cut off from everyone.

A few days after Mrs. Shepherd called asking for our address, I received a life-changing letter from Andrew's father. Apparently, Mrs. Shepherd had given him our new address. The letter said:

My dearest Kathryn,

I am sorry to inform you that Andrew and four other soldiers in his unit have been killed in the line of duty. As you know, Andrew's mother, Juliette has not been well for several years, and when she got word about Andrew's death, she suffered a debilitating stroke and she can no longer speak or walk.

Word of Andrew's death was just too much for her. She is now bed-ridden and I have been forced to place her in a care facility. I have been by her side every day since the stroke, but I feel so helpless. The doctors have not given me much hope for her recovery. Between the loss of Andrew and Juliette's illness, I feel like someone needs to stand over me and remind me to breathe. Andrew and Juliette were all I had. They were my whole world.

Everything has crashed down around me. I sit in my front room, and stare at the walls. I haven't gone to work since Juliette had her stroke, and I haven't felt like talking to anyone. Please forgive me for not notifying you earlier. The past few weeks have been overwhelming and I am not sure how I can go on.

The Vietnam War has hit home to many other families in Arlington too. First, we received word about Andrew and his unit, and then some other families got word of the deaths of their sons, we lost Johnny Johnson, Dwayne Reiner, Mark Jamison, and another young man named Randall Bose from the Boston area. The entire region is in mourning.

I am so sorry to have to share such horrendous news with you sweet Kathryn, but Jane Shepherd told me you had been trying to contact us about Andrew. I knew it was time to let you know. My heart is broken, and I can barely get out if bed each morning.

Go live your life Kathryn, and never forget how much you were loved by our son, and by Juliette and me.

Sincerely,

Andrew Paul Brookshire II

I read his letter over again. Andrew along with four other soldiers in his unit are dead, and my lifelong friends Johnny, Dwayne and Mark were also killed. "No, no this can't be happening," I screamed to the top of my lungs.

My mother came running from the kitchen, just as I tossed the letter at Keith to read, and then I ran upstairs to my bedroom and flung myself face down on my bed, and wailed into my Andrew bear.

Within a few minutes, my mom and Keith came up to my room, my mother put her arms around both of us, and we all three hugged each other and uncontrollably sobbed. This was just too much for us to endure. We had been happily setting up a new life in Idaho while our friends back home in Arlington were suffering and dying.

We had continually heard on the television how horrible the war was, but we had no idea how shocking it could truly be. It didn't seem real. How could we possibly lose four young men from our High School graduation class: Andrew, Johnny, Mark, and Dwayne. I instantly thought of all the families; families that I had known all my life. Families that we had gone to church with; families who had now lost their sons forever.

My poor brother Keith was just shaking and sobbing incessantly. Johnny and Mark had been his best friends since they were all in kindergarten. They were part of his entire childhood, and all his church and school memories. They played football together. They ate lunch together every day since grade school, and he will never see then again.

My mom kept her arms wrapped around Keith and me for almost an hour. Then she got up to go and call my dad. She wanted to tell him about the letter from Andrew's father. I glanced at Keith staring out of my bedroom window, and for one second, I realized it could have been Keith along with Andrew, Mark and Johnny who were killed in Vietnam. Because he tried to enlist with them, but was unable to go.

I walked over and gently put my arms around his shoulders and kissed the top of his head, because I knew he was hurting just as much as I was. In that instant, I realized what Andrew's dad had said about not knowing how to go on, and needing to be told to breathe. He told me to go live my life, but my life was Andrew. Since I was thirteen years old, Andrew was the love of my life....MY FOREVER LOVE.

Seven

God Had a Different Plan

The next few months were just empty. I went about my day quietly surviving. I wore my heart necklace that Andrew had given me, and each night I continued to repeat my memory verse after I said my prayers. 1 Thessalonians 5:16-18, Rejoice always, pray continually, give thanks in all circumstances; for this is God's will for you in Christ Jesus. I knew that even if Andrew were gone, he would always remain alive within my heart.

When winter came, Keith and I learned how to snow ski. It seemed like everyone in the Boise valley could ski. Bogus Basin was right up the road from our house. It was directly up Harrison Boulevard, in the mountains about twenty miles away. We took skiing lessons for several weeks, and between school and lessons, it really helped us get through such a confusing time.

Every day we would hear of another young soldier losing his life to the devastating Viet Nam War. Families were torn apart, and children were left without Fathers. I silently prayed each time I heard of another soldier not coming home. Yet, the ones that were coming home were ridiculed, and called baby killers. Many had nightmares, some survived by drinking, others just couldn't adjust to being back with their families again. It was a terrifying time in our nation's history.

I continued to attend college with intentions to become a nurse one day. I realized that all my plans about marrying Andrew, and being a minister's wife, living in Arlington and having four children would never be. I needed to go in a different direction, and nursing seemed like a good option.

I never heard from Andrew's father or Mrs. Shepherd again. Our family realized that our old life back in Arlington was irreversibly over, and it was time to move on. While Keith was still in college, he started working at my father's office. Keith was taking accounting courses with plans to one day be an accountant for the business. My dad loved having Keith work with him, and it was excellent job training for Keith to be a part of such a successful company.

My mother soon joined up with a large interior decorating firm. Within that first year she became one of the firm's partners. They had a beautiful office downtown. Now that we were grown, she was free to work away from home, and spend the time focused on her professional skills and talents.

In late Spring, the college had a school dance and Keith and his girlfriend Margie convinced me to go with them. The room was decorated in beautiful colors, and the students were partying like they didn't have a care in the world. I danced several dances, and it felt good to feel somewhat alive again.

Then suddenly I realized that one year ago tonight, Andrew and I were crowned the Prom King and Queen of our High School. I shook my head in disbelief, because it had been such a horrendous year. Things had gone so differently than any of us had ever imagined it would go. It was hard to believe that it had only been one year ago, that my world was perfect, if only for that one night. I still felt numb inside, but I was slowly learning to survive, and I rarely cried myself to sleep anymore.

I somehow got through my second year of college, and the next summer, I decided to take a special summer school class to learn more about the nursing program. The class was led by a young doctor by the name of Dr. Samuel Peterson. He was so interesting, and he was an excellent teacher. It was a six-week course and Dr. Peterson was extremely knowledgeable. His summer class got me more and more excited about becoming an office nurse. Dr. Peterson truly believed in helping people, and he communicated his enthusiasm to everyone in the group.

I thoroughly enjoyed the class, and I ask Dr. Peterson a lot of questions, because he explained things so well. One day, he told me that I was his star student, because I was so interested in everything that he said. After the six-week course was over, Dr. Peterson surprised me and asked me out to lunch. My first response was to say no, but I knew that he wasn't married and that even being a doctor, he wasn't that much older than me. I truly respected him as a teacher, and I thought he was nice, so for some reason I told him yes. I hadn't dated anyone since Andrew left for Vietnam, and I realized that maybe it was time for me to move forward with my life.

It had been over two years since Andrew left, and I had never heard from his father again. In a few months Keith and I would have our 21st birthday, so maybe it was time to start living life again. I had never noticed how handsome Dr. Peterson was, until he grinned his gorgeous smile at me and ask me to go to lunch. He was about 6 foot 3, with a soft baby face, and a very slender build. He had dark-brown hair and big brown eyes. He was the complete opposite of my Andrew.

We had lunch downtown at a nice restaurant called the Royal Restaurant. It was quiet and we had time to talk. I learned that Dr. Samuel Dean Peterson was 26 years old, and he had never been married, because he had concentrated the past few years on getting through medical school and setting up his practice. He told me he dated a lot in high school, but he hadn't dated anyone since he started medical school.

Dr. Peterson was a good listener. I told him all about my plans to marry Andrew and to be a minister's wife, and have four children. Of course, I also told him about Andrew and several of my friends leaving Arlington, Massachusetts for Vietnam right after graduation, and never coming home. I showed him my necklace and told him that I never take it off.

He was so gentle and easy to talk to, it seemed we could talk about anything. We sat in the restaurant for over two hours and just got to know each other. He said, "I could tell that you had been gravely hurt by something, because of how reserved and serious you are. You are much more mature than most of the other college girls in the class."

I told him, "I lived in Arlington, Massachusetts for most of my life." I grinned as I told him, "I am a twin, and my brother Keith has always been my best friend." I innocently told him, "I play the piano and sing and I have recently learned to snow ski." For some reason I even told him that I felt our parents had brought us clear across America to Idaho, to start a new life.

He told me, "I have lived in Idaho most of my life, except when I went away to medical school. I have one brother and one sister, who are both married and live in Boise. My brother has three children, and my sister has one brand-new baby, that I love to babysit. My mom is a stay-at-home mom, my dad and my grandpa were both small-town doctors, that is why I wanted to be a doctor."

He smiled and said, "I attend a Christian Church, out on the bench, and I own a house about three blocks from the church. I share an office with two other doctors on Bannock Street in downtown Boise. I play guitar, I sing in the church choir, and I love a good barbecued steak, with corn on-the-cob, and a big baked potato." He sheepishly stated, "Maybe you can come over one day next week, and I can barbecue some steaks."

I didn't answer, I just smiled and sort of nodded my head up and down. I had to admit I thoroughly enjoyed the entire afternoon. It was one of the nicest days that I have had since Andrew left. Samuel was kind, smart, calm, honest and easy to be with. As confusing as my life had been in the past two years, he made me feel like a normal person again.

After I left the restaurant that day, I felt hopeful for the first time in almost two years. The dark cloud above my head was slightly clearing. Samuel Peterson was a few years older than I was, but maybe that is just what I needed to help me move on with my life. Until today I had no future.

The very next week he invited me, along with my brother Keith and his fiancé, Margie over for dinner. Samuel had a beautiful home out on the bench, and he fixed us some fantastic barbecued steaks out on his backyard patio. Keith and Samuel hit it off right away because they had so much in common. They talked about football, basketball, playing guitars, hiking and snow skiing at Bogus Basin and Sun Valley, Idaho. Keith, Margie, and I left around 12:30 that night after making plans to float down the Boise River the next Saturday.

In all the time that we had lived in Boise, we had never floated down the Boise River, but we had heard people talk about it many times. We were excited for this fun new adventure. Sam took the four of us on several outings over the next few months. He had lived in Boise most of his life, and he could hardly wait to share Idaho's great outdoors with us.

We went to concerts in the park and rode bicycles along the river. The four of us went hiking in the foothills, and water skied at Lucky Peak Reservoir with Margie's family boat. We played tennis at the college, went to the museums, walked the beautiful Rose Gardens, and rode paddle wheels at Julia Davis Park.

At the end of the school year, I got my nursing degree and went to work as a beginning nurse in Sam's clinic. There were three other nurses that worked in the center. It was a nice office that Sam shared with two other doctors. One of the other doctor's wives had decorated it, and made it modern and inviting. Between the three doctors they had a great practice going.

Dr. Sam Peterson and I had been seeing each other for almost a year when he asked me to marry him. He was such a wonderful man, he was handsome, gentle, intelligent, and fun to be around. As confused as my life had been before I met him, it was refreshing to be with someone who was older and more settled. He owned a home, he was an established doctor, he had become best friends with my brother Keith, my parents adored him, and I knew he truly loved me. So, we planned a wedding for June 8th.

As wonderful as the past year had been, I still felt confusion about Andrew. I had never taken off ‘My Forever Love’ necklace, and of course Samuel knew it. I had worn the necklace continually for the past three years, but I was confused as to what I should I do with it now that I was marrying someone else?

The week before the wedding I got more and more confused, and Samuel could tell it. He sat me down and looked directly into my eyes and said, “Kathryn, I know how much that necklace means to you. I know that Andrew was your first love, and you are such a loyal, loving person. That is why I fell in love with you, so I will never ask you to take it off.” He put his arms around me and held me close and said, “Maybe one day you will feel like it is time, but I will never ask you to take it off because of me.” He smiled, “It will be enough just to have you as my wife.”

Keith and Margie were married that April, and Sam and I got married in June. Our parents had two large weddings within two months, but they were so glad to have the both of us settled and happy. I had to admit my dad was right, moving to Idaho was a great idea for all of us.

A short time after our first wedding anniversary, Sam talked with me about going to South Africa with him and some other doctors for a program called ‘Doctors Without Borders.’ It is a private international association founded to provide assistance to populations of victims of natural disasters or man-made disasters, or victims of conflict. They help people irrespective of race, religion, creed, or political beliefs. Most of the doctors that are a part of the MSF or 'Doctors Without Borders' are family physicians like Samuel. They provide health services in areas of the world that are too dangerous for other non-profit medical health agencies to work in.

Sam wanted me to go to South Africa with him as a nurse to help the people learn how to read, and to give mass vaccinations. Many young married couples were part of the 'Doctors Without Borders' group. Most couples teamed up and were gone for 9 to 12 months. I was excited to share this mission with Sam, this had been a dream of his since he started medical school. We made arrangements to leave in October with plans to return to the states in August.

Five weeks before we were to leave, we discovered that I was pregnant with our first child. I was strong, healthy, and feeling fine, but the MSF program would not let me go to South Africa with my husband because it was not a safe environment, especially for someone pregnant.

We were both disappointed that I would not be allowed to go, but I encouraged Sam to go on ahead with the other doctors. I knew how badly he wanted to be part of the team. This was a dream-come-true for him, and I didn't want to destroy his dream just because I couldn't go. So, he changed his plans from being gone ten months to only five months and then he could return to the states in plenty of time to be here for the arrival of the baby. There was no reason that he could not go without me. I had my parents, Sam's parents, and Keith and Margie to help me if I needed anything. I would be fine and we knew that he would be back in plenty of time to deliver the baby.

I convinced him that this might be his only opportunity to go with the other doctors, because once we start our family, I knew he would never go overseas and leave us. He was a good, kind man, always ready to help others, but he was also a very devoted husband to me, and I knew that he wouldn't go if I didn't encourage him.

I was truly happy for him to live out this part of his life's plan. As the day approached for him to leave, he got more and more excited about going to South Africa to help the people. Sam was a good-natured person, who was always smiling, but I had never seen him as happy as he was the day he left for South Africa.

He was ecstatic to be heading off half-way around the world on this extraordinary adventure. Sam was such an accomplished person. He had done so much in his life for being so young. He always worked hard and this would be something remarkable that we could one day tell our grandchildren about.

I kissed him goodbye and happily waved and took pictures of him and all the doctors as they boarded the huge plane for their long flight. I stood there with Sam's parents, Melvin and Victoria, his brother and his family, and his sister and her family, and of course my parents, and Keith and Margie. Everyone was so pleased to be there to see the doctors off, and I could not be more-proud of my husband as I watched him and the other doctors flying off to fulfill their dreams. Only a few doctors were traveling to South Africa at that time because most of the MSF doctors had already gone to the Cambodia-Thai border to care for people fleeing the Khmer Rouge regime.

Within two days, I received a long-distance phone call from South Africa. It was Sam telling us that he had safely arrived. He said, "The rainy season has started a little early, and it is really wet and muggy." He sounded exhausted after the long flight, but he was still very upbeat and excited, as he said, "Tomorrow we will head to our selected destination, it is a small remote impoverished village, and I may have difficulty sending mail or making phone calls, but I will contact you as often as possible."

While Sam was gone to Africa, my mother and I got busy preparing the baby's room. I decided to paint it yellow with white trim. That way it would be fresh and clean for either a boy or a girl. My mom was so excited to have her first grandchild, she went shopping almost every day. She bought every kind of stuffed animal the toy store had.

Since I didn't go with Sam, there was no reason for the office to hire another nurse to replace me. I just planned to continue working at the clinic until Sam returned from Africa, but I did change my schedule to part-time. There was no reason to stay home all day, the other doctors were there, and the clinic was open, and I wanted to stay busy to help the time go faster.

About four weeks after I received the first phone call from Sam, I received a letter from him telling me all about the projects the doctors were doing there. He wrote ten pages sharing the inexhaustible events he had witnessed in the flooded tiny village where the doctors had been working.

Sam told me the doctors were near Musina, South Africa the northernmost agricultural area, along the Zimbabwe border. It was a very remote region with precarious working conditions and long distances from any type of health facilities. The doctors of the MSF program were to provide emergency medicine, response to epidemics, help with nutritional and vaccinations, and operate a feeding center for malnourished children.

He told me of the horrible living conditions that the people endured, and of the widespread starvation throughout the small remote community. Samuel wrote that the death and sickness was overwhelming, but he was so pleased that he was there to help them. He said he worked ten hours each day, and he was very tired, but he truly felt they were making a difference.

South Africa was still living under the laws of the Apartheid System when Sam and the doctors were there. Apartheid was a system of institutionalized racial segregation that existed in South Africa and South West Africa. It was policies that governed relationships between South Africans, white minorities, and non-white majorities for much of the latter half of the 20th Century.

The implementation of Apartheid, is often called, 'Separate Development.' The Bantu Homelands Citizenship Act of 1970 made every black South African, irrespectively of actual residence a citizen of the Bantustans, which were organized based on ethnic and linguistic groupings by white leaders. Blacks were stripped of their South African citizenship. The black Africans had been removed from their homes and forced into segregated neighborhoods. It was some of the largest mass evictions in modern history. The black people would lose their South African citizenship as they were absorbed into the Bantustans.

The South African government manipulated homeland policies so that the 'complaint chiefs' controlled the administrations of most of the territories. South Africa was dominated politically, socially, and economically by the nation's minority white population. The social system was said to have status, with white citizens first. Apartheid entitled the segregation of public facilities and social events, which dictated housing and employment opportunities by race. They declared Black people as aliens in urban areas.

Sam was such a charitable person, and he truly felt sorry for the victimized black families that had come to the doctors for help from the fragmented surrounding territories. Many people would walk for miles to see the American doctors, because they knew they would sincerely try to help them and their families. Sam wrote page after page sharing the things that his team had been doing since they arrived in the small village.

Over the next few weeks, I got several letters from Sam. Each letter got shorter and shorter, and he sounded more exhausted with each one I received. He told me, "Working in this muddy, damp environment has really helped me to appreciate the clean, modern, comfort of living in America. Although we have tents to work under, it seems we are usually standing ankle deep in wet, sloppy mud. The rain is so heavy it often runs under the tent sides." He said, "And the bugs, I do not think I will ever get used to the bugs. The giant beetles, the termites, and the mosquitoes."

He sincerely said, "It is hard to believe that this part of the world is so opposite of our peaceful, joyful life and abundant freedoms. Africa has made me appreciate how truly blessed our lives are." He sadly admitted, "It seems we help one dying child, and still three other children starve to death right before our eyes."

In one of the latest letters, Sam told me, "I am glad I have been able to come to Africa to help with the work of the MSF, but I will be ready to return when my five months is over. Kathryn, you have given me such a beautiful life, and I can hardly wait to have our first child, and make our perfect world complete."

His letter was sweet, and I was happy for him to be able to live out his dream working with the MSF, but I could tell that he was ready to come home. He was such a family person and it was hard for him to be so far away from all of us. We had already spent Halloween, Thanksgiving, the

Christmas holidays, New Year's Day, and Valentine's Day apart so I looked forward to him coming back for Easter.

Everything was going fine at home, and I knew he would be back in the states within a couple of months. I had been to my OB/GYN a few days earlier and he felt the pregnancy was going well. I was tired all the time, but at least the morning sickness had passed. The doctor was a little surprised at how quickly the baby was growing, but it had a strong heartbeat and I hadn't had any real complications at all.

The days passed quickly. Finally, it was only about three weeks until Sam was to get back in the country. I had just gotten home from shopping with my mom when I received another letter from Sam. This time it was a letter mailed by Global Express Service. Apparently, Sam had been taken to a hospital for treatment.

The letter said:

My dearest Kathryn,

The entire team has contacted malaria and I am sad to say I just lost my dear friend and colleague Dr. Robert Wilton. We are all very sick, and they are taking us by truck to Johannesburg to a hospital. I wanted to let you know how thankful I am that you became my wife. I could never have asked for a more beautiful, kind, Godly woman to be my spouse. As a doctor, I know that I am very ill. I know that I will soon be in a coma. I am afraid Kathryn, and I fear that the Lord might call me home even before you receive this letter.

I looked so forward to having a family, but I sincerely regret that I will never get the opportunity to meet my son or my daughter. May the Lord surround you in His loving arms over the next few months.

Always remember how much you were loved.

Sam

I almost fainted; I couldn't believe what I was reading. Luckily my mother was standing by my side as I read Sam's goodbye letter. Since Sam was out of the country, my mother and I often went shopping in the afternoon. We had stopped for a leisurely lunch, and to look at baby beds before coming home. We did not have a worry in the world, until now.

I buried my face in my hands and screamed, "No, no, no this cannot be happening. Not Sam too." I looked up at my mother, then covered my face and cried. Like with Andrew, my mother wrapped her arms around me, and kind of rocked me back and forth and cried with me. We were both in shock.

After a few minutes, she got up and called my dad's office. She wanted my Father to get ahold of the MSF office (The Doctors without Borders), and try to contact the hospital in South Africa where Sam was taken.

About four hours later, we received confirmation that both Dr. Samuel Peterson and Dr. Robert Wilton had both died from kidney failure, as the result of Malaria. A third doctor, Dr. James Smithson seemed to be getting better after his hospital treatments. My father was told that it had taken several days to get the doctors out of the remote village where they had been working. It was summer in the region, but the roads had been washed away by the torrential afternoon downpours, which made traveling very slow and tedious. We were told that perhaps they could have all survived if they had arrived at the hospital earlier.

My Father was given the name of a missionary who had helped bring the three doctors to the hospital when they got sick. My dad contacted the missionary personally and he said that he had been the person who had sent the Global Express letter that Sam had written. He told us that Sam had written the letter to his beloved wife on the way down from the village, right before he went into a coma.

He mailed the letter for Sam as a personal favor because he said, "The wonderful doctor had saved the life of my wife, just two months earlier." The man, Brent Anderson said that he and his wife, Carla were missionaries from Sheridan, Wyoming. They had been sent to the village to be missionaries about seven months ago, and they had become good friends with all the doctors. He told my dad that Sam had done an emergency appendectomy, on his wife, eight weeks ago, in the middle of the night, and the surgery had saved her life.

Mr. Anderson said, "The other doctor, Dr. Wilton had already passed away when I left to send Sam's letter to America." He said, "I helped Sam write the letter to his wife as we were riding in the back of the truck on the way to the hospital." He sadly added, "I was afraid that Sam's wife would never get the letter if I didn't personally send it to the states myself." The man was crying as he told my father, "Sam was a good Christian man, and a good friend, and he had helped so many people in the village; sending his letter was the least I could do."

Over the next few days, my OB/GYN doctor gave me something so that I could rest, because he was concerned about the pregnancy. Within the week, Sam's body was sent back to the states so we could have a proper funeral for him. It was a huge funeral; Sam had so many people that loved and admired him. He had church friends, his patients, other doctors, people involved in MSF, school friends and of course all his family. The entire funeral, and the days that followed were a complete disorientation for me.

Through all the months that Sam was in South Africa, I never feared that he wouldn't come home to me. He wanted so badly to live out this dream, and I was just patiently waiting at home for his return. It never once entered my mind that when he got on that plane with the other doctors, that I would never see him again.

A few days after the funeral, my parents went with me as I talked with our lawyer. Sam had all his affairs in order, before he left for South Africa. He had taken care of everything. He was always so organized and proper. He left a large insurance policy plus providing for the house, car, and immediate bills to be paid in full.

For the next few weeks, I walked around in disbelief and total confusion, and my OB/GYN doctor was very concerned about me. He wanted me to spend most of my time resting for the last several weeks of my pregnancy. I had been through such an emotional loss, he feared the baby might come early, and he wanted me to carry it as long as possible.

One afternoon, I went to the closet and dug out the bear that Andrew had given me right before he left for Vietnam. I once again buried my face into the soft cuddly fur, I squeezed it tightly and mourned the loss of both Andrew and Sam. I silently repeated the memory verse: 1 Thessalonians 5: 16-18, Rejoice always, pray continually, give thanks in all circumstances; for this is God's will for you in Christ Jesus.

My mind was overcome with grief, but I followed the doctor's orders and I rested most of the day. My mom and my sister-in-law Margie took turns spending time with me during the daylight hours, and every night either my brother Keith, my dad, or Sam's mother, Victoria would stay with me and sleep in the guest room so that I would not be alone. I barely remember the days that followed Sam's funeral, so I was lucky to have so many family members around to help me get through that time.

Luckily, it was my mom that was with me the afternoon my water broke. I wasn't due for another two weeks, but with all the stress I had been through, I guess I was lucky to have carried the baby as long as I did.

My mom drove me to Saint Luke's Hospital in downtown Boise, that was the hospital that delivered babies. At that time Saint Alphonsus Hospital took care of older patients, and Saint Luke's Hospital had pediatrics.

When I got to the hospital, they quickly checked me in, then raced me directly into the delivery room where my doctor was already waiting. As sad as I had been over the past few weeks, I suddenly realized this was really happening, I was going to have a baby.

I was only in the delivery room for a few minutes when the nurse stood by my side and told me to push. I took short breathes and listened to the nurse's instructions. The pain was almost unbearable, and then I heard the faint cry of my newborn son. Within a few seconds the cry got louder and stronger and they placed the tiny newborn on my chest.

A short time later I heard the doctor say in a surprised voice, "Oh No." Just then I felt another unbearable sharp pain, the nurse whisked the first baby away as the doctor prepared for baby boy number two to be delivered. Suddenly, I was no longer all alone in this world. I was blessed with twin boys. I once again closed my eyes and silently repeated: 1 Thessalonians 5:16-18, Rejoice always, pray continually, give thanks in all circumstances; for this is God's will for you in Christ Jesus.

Eight
The Twins

I loved being a mommy, it was one the greatest blessings the Lord had ever given me. My boys were healthy and strong and they kept me busy from morning till night. I was too busy to even think about all my sadness from the past several years. I had family that continually helped me, and surprisingly I had to admit, it was one the most joyful times in my life. I had never dreamed I would be a single mother with twins, but between my mom and Sam's mom I always had a grandma there to help with the boys.

My mother went on leave from her job a few days after we received Sam's goodbye letter, so she could faithfully be there to help me. The grandparents were such a great help, especially the first few weeks. Someone stayed with me all the time. We had enough relatives that they only needed to help me a few hours each day, then someone else would come along to replace them so that they could go home. My mom, my dad or Victoria and Melvin, my brother Keith, my sister-in-law Margie, and of course Sam's brother and sister. They all loved the twins almost as much as I did.

Sam had left me financially very comfortable, so I could stay home and raise our sons, and I would never need to work again. I knew that I could always go back into nursing once the boys were grown.

One of my favorite times of the day was after I put the boys to bed at night. I would stand over them and just praise the Lord for how perfect they were. Sam would be so proud of his two handsome young men. It always amazed me how much both boys looked like their father. Sam was tall and handsome, and the boys had his sweet baby face, his thick, dark hair, and big brown eyes, and they were identical twins.

They were such a joy. I cherished every day of their life, because every day was a new day. Just watching them learn to coo, roll over, crawl, then learn to walk, and learn to talk seemed like a miracle from God. From the time they were three months old, I took them out every single day in a double stroller, and we would go for a long, brisk walk. Even as the weather grew cooler, I would bundle them up, and we would get out in the clean fresh air and take our walks. The three of us were inseparable. My two little men were my life.

The boys were about 18 months old when a woman from my church asked me if I would come and sing and play the piano, then speak at a lady's luncheon and share my testimony. It seemed the Vietnam war had affected so many people in America, in so many ways. People had lost husbands, sons, fathers, daughters, neighbors, and other family members. Along with everything else that had happened in my lifetime, I soon discovered that people appreciated hearing my story.

That was the beginning of a whole new life for me, from that day on I talked at Christian women's groups throughout Idaho and the surrounding area. I prayed that perhaps my survival autobiography would encourage other women to get through the heartache and problems that they might be dealing with. I wanted people to know my Jesus. I personally knew that without my strong belief in God I couldn't have gotten through the things that I have lived through.

I began every speaking engagement with 1 Thessalonians 5:16-18, the verse that Andrew had given to me the day that he left for Vietnam. That verse was my strength, my hope, and my vision. It is the verse that I lived by, it was the verse that has kept me going through all my fears and trials.

1 Thessalonians 5:16-18, Rejoice always. Rejoicing always is the hardest of all the verses. It is hard to rejoice when your heart is broken, and you have no idea how you will get through even one more day. It is hard to rejoice when you can see no plan for a future. To rejoice when everything is dark and hopeless. That is the hardest thing in life to try to do.

Pray continually. That has been the easiest verse for me, because it has always been easy for me to pray and talk to my Lord. I can pray wherever I am or whatever I am doing. At my lowest moments of my life, I could just close my eyes and talk to God. He is my closest friend. He understands when no one else can.

Give thanks in all circumstances; for this is God's will for you in Christ Jesus. Oftentimes in my lifetime it has been hard for me to give thanks, because everything seemed so hopeless and I could see no end in sight. Yet, somehow, I would wake up in the morning, and the sun would start shining, and I could once again give thanks. I would often conclude my speeches by reading my goodbye letter that Sam had written to me right before he died. Then I would share short stories about raising my handsome young twin boys.

I began to get invitations to speak from several Christian organizations throughout the valley. I would always sing and play the piano before I gave my testimony, and I soon found myself speaking and singing in huge auditoriums, and massive convention centers. I enjoyed performing and telling my story, but I found myself living a hectic new life that I never dreamed I would be living. I would often speak to thousands of people at Christian seminars, both men and women. Sometimes I would almost have to pinch myself when I stopped to realize what all the Lord had brought me through, just so I could share my story with so many people. So much of my life had been filled with sorrow, yet at 27 years old I felt truly blessed.

My mother or my mother-in-law would graciously watch the twins while I was busy speaking, but I was rarely gone for more than a few hours during the day, or a couple of hours in the evening. If I needed to go out of town to speak, either my mother or my mother-in-law would travel with me to watch the boys. My life had taken on such a different twist than I ever envisioned it would to be. I had dreamed of a simple, easy life as a happily married wife with several children, a beautiful family home with a big backyard. Yet, instead I was an active public speaker, Bible study leader and single mother of twins.

Although, my life had gone through so many adversities over the past few years, I could have never imagined how wonderful and fulfilled it could now be. I was forced to become a strong single mother. I loved my singing and speaking engagements, I loved my boys, I loved my family, I loved my church, and I enjoyed my active life.

The boys had their two grandpas, they had my brother and of course Sam's brother as male role models, but sometimes at night the sadness would still come over me that the boys would never have a father, and I knew boys needed a father. I watched Keith working alongside my dad and I admired the special father-son relationship that they had. I knew my boys would never have that special bond that Keith had with my dad. And of course, all the other little boys that lived in the neighborhood had dads, and all their friends at church had both their mother and their father.

Financially, we had everything that we needed. I taught weekly Bible studies and spoke to groups at least once a month. The boys were now three years old, and I put them in a Christian pre-school two mornings a week. We still took our daily walks, and we often met at the park for playdates with friends from church.

We had our family nearby; the boys were healthy and growing taller every day. We were very busy all the time, but as hard as I tried to be both parents, I still sometimes felt our world was incomplete. I missed Samuel so much, he was such a kind, and gentle husband, and he would have been such a wonderful father to his boys.

After all the times I had talked to groups about surviving through of the sorrows of my life, and appearing to be so happy, contented, and brave, I silently struggled with loneliness. Frequently late at night, when I was all alone praying, I quietly mourned the disappointment of never having a normal marriage and family, and the loss of my forever love. I do not believe the deep pain of loss ever truly goes away.

Nine
Gone to the Mountains

In March, Keith and I both received an invitation to our 10-year class reunion. Ten years, I couldn't believe it had been 10 years since we graduated and had left Arlington. My first response was, "Oh I am just too busy to go. That is such a long trip, it is thousands of miles from Idaho."

Yet, the real reason was I felt such deep sadness when I thought about my High School class. We had lost so many friends after we graduated, besides who would we even go to see? It made my heart ache to think about graduation, because I had loved High School so much. I treasured those years. I felt tears once again trickling down my face. Even after ten years and everything that has happened in my life, I still missed Andrew so much. I mourned for the loss of our dreams, our hopes, and our life together. I bowed my head and covered my face and caught myself automatically saying 1 Thessalonians 5:15-18, as I placed my hand around my heart necklace and clutched it to my neck. I had never taken it off in ten years. I had worn it privately inside my clothes, ever since the day that Andrew had put it around my neck.

Instantly, I could again feel the deep sorrow and the crushing agony of Andrew leaving for war and never coming home again. I closed my eyes and it felt like yesterday. I could still picture Andrew with his beautiful blue eyes, his handsome imposing face, and his strong arms as he held me close, and put 'MY FOREVER LOVE' heart necklace around my neck.

I began to sob as I clearly heard his voice say, "Wear this, and never take it off, until we are together again." I covered my face and tried to hold back the tears, but it still seemed so real, I could not stop the uncontrollable torment that I felt. I went to the closet and took out our High School prom picture that was taken just a few weeks before he left. I kept it in a box on the top shelf of the spare bedroom. I stared at the young good-looking couple smiling in the picture. We held the world in our hands, and I am so thankful that I had my Andrew, if only for a short time, he was such a blessing to me.

I suddenly realized, that it does not really matter how far away you run, even if you are clear on the other side of the United States, or across the ocean, gone off to war. The unconditional love and memories are always with you, hidden deep inside your heart, as if it were just yesterday.

Keith called me when he received his invitation, and ask me if I wanted to go. I quickly told him, "I would love to see Arlington again, but I do not think I am strong enough to face all the memories. Keith, everything I cared about died the day Andrew, Mark, and Johnny got on that plane to leave for Vietnam, and never came home." We both decided it was probably be best not to go.

For several days after I received the invitation, I was haunted with memories from the past. Happy memories, fun memories, the good times, church camp, basketball games, football games, going to proms, singing in school assemblies with Andrew ...my youth, but I still did not feel up to going to the class reunion.

The Vietnam War ended on March 29, 1973, but for me like so many other people who had lost someone, it would never really end. Because a big part of our lives would forever be left behind with our loved ones in the Vietnam war.

Ten years had passed since we graduated from High School and so many things had happened just this year: President Jimmy Carter had pardoned the Vietnam draft dodgers so that they could go home. Elvis Pressley performed his final concert in Indiana and died a short time later in Graceland at the age of 42. The movie 'Star Wars' first appeared in movie theaters. We had Super Bowl XI won by the Oakland Raiders. Snow falls in Miami, Florida. The Dallas Cowboys, defeat the Denver Broncos. The NASA space shuttle named 'Enterprise' makes its first flight from the back of a Boeing

747 shuttle carrier aircraft. John Travolta's role in Saturday Night Fever inspired young Americans to wear Flare jeans. The New York City Blackout lasted 25 hours. British Airways inaugurates regular London to New York City supersonic Concorde service. The comic strip 'Lil Abner' ends after 43 years in the newspaper.

As I sat there and pondered all the things that have happened in the world in the past few months, I could not help but feel it was not fair. So many of us who have lost loved ones in the last several years are still all alone, yet the world goes on.

Sunday night, four days after I received the invitation to the reunion, I once again had the dream about Andrew and I standing up in front of the church and getting married. It was such a vivid dream, a comforting dream; until I woke with a jolt and started screaming out loud, because I realized I was dreaming, and I remembered Andrew was gone. I buried my face into my pillow, trying not to wake the twins, and cried with my face buried in my pillow for hours until I finally cried myself back to sleep.

Each night for the next three nights, I had the same recurring dream about Andrew and I getting married. By the fourth night I was almost afraid to go to bed, so I took a sleeping pill so I could sleep, and I slept all through the night. I was so stressed out; I knew the invitation to our ten-year class reunion had brought up all the horrifying recollections from the past. Yet, I couldn't seem to get the amazing memories of that time out of my head either.

The next day my mother received a first-class certified letter, that was sent to her house with my name on it. She signed for it and brought it to me to open. The return address was from Andrew's father in Arlington.

The letter said:

My dearest Kathryn,

I should have contacted you before now, but a few years ago when I decided to get in touch with you, I found out you were engaged to marry a local doctor so I did not call. Just recently I received word that you had twin boys, and that your husband had passed away.

With your ten-year class reunion coming up, I knew it was finally time for me to contact you. Kathryn, so many confusing things have happened in the past several years that I don't even know where to begin.

When I last wrote to you, we had just buried our only son, your beloved Andrew. My wife Juliette was very ill and was living in a nursing home. I made special arrangements for Juliette to attend Andrew's funeral, but she was unable to talk or even sit up. I had to make all the funeral preparations for Andrew, on my own.

Juliette died just two weeks after Andrew's funeral and my whole existence went into a deep depression. I was unaware of anything around me. At first, I slept in my truck, and then somehow, I found my way up the mountain to our family cabin.

The cabin is high up in the mountains, at the end of the road. There are no other cabins around for miles. I had no contact with anyone for several months. I had no phone, no mail, I felt I had no reason to talk to anyone because my world had been buried with Andrew and Juliette.

I ate only enough to keep alive. Juliette had stored canned goods in the cabin, so that is what I lived on. I never changed my clothes or shaved. I did not bathe or cut my hair. I just existed. The cabin has power, water, and sewer so I was able to survive. I never once went back to the house. I didn't have any reason to go home, there was nothing there.

Juliette was my high school sweetheart; she was my only true love, and I loved her with my entire being. And I was so proud of Andrew, he had grown into such a good, kind, honest and thoughtful person. He was so proper and he always did what was right.

I liked my job, we all treasured our church, we liked living in Arlington, we enjoyed our friends and our neighbors. The three of us absolutely loved our lives. I cannot believe how perfect our life was, but when I buried Andrew and Juliette, I had lost all reason to live.

After I was gone for a few days, the mailman began hiding my mail away for me. He had been our mailman for many years and he knew if we were gone, he could put our mail, in a large metal box inside the fence, in the backyard. All the bills at the house got behind, the house payment, utilities, everything was neglected. But because I had been the president of the bank for the past 16 years, my vice president, Howard Phillips, safeguarded my expenses, he contacted my accountant so he could take care of my finances. The bank put me on paid sick leave for several months. They knew I would take care of things when I got back on my feet. My entire world was just devastated.

Juliette, Andrew, and I had lived in our house for years, everyone around the neighborhood knew that I had lost both Andrew and Juliette, so they were all very gracious about keeping everything on hold until I was ready to come back. The neighbors kept watch on the house and they even mowed the lawn and collected the newspaper. One close neighbor had even driven all the way up to the cabin to make sure I was still alive. He did not bother me, but at least the neighbors and my bank employees knew where I was and that I was alright. Everyone just gave me my private time to mourn my unbearable loss.

I cannot imagine a darker time in my life. I sat inside the cabin day after day and tried to figure out how to move forward. I still had a job, and all the material things that we had accumulated throughout our married lifetime, but nothing had any purpose. When you lose the people you love, you have lost it all.

I did not leave the mountain for several months. When I finally decided I was strong enough to go back home, I couldn't get even my truck started. It hadn't been started for so long, the battery was dead. There was no one around to help me so I charged the battery for 24 hours with a slow battery charger, and the truck finally started and I cautiously headed towards home.

The closer I got to town the more apprehensive I became. I had been gone from civilization for so long, I wasn't sure what to expect. I knew that I smelled terrible, I was filthy and I looked like a wild mountain man. I did not know for sure how much weight I had lost, but I knew I had lost quite a bit. My clothes were hanging on me. I had completely shutout the outside world because there was nothing, I was interested in. I hadn't heard any news or read a newspaper for months. My mind had been on total withdrawal, that is the only way I could survive.

As I think back now, it is still hard for me to comprehend that I had been completely out of touch with everyone for so long. You cannot believe that your entire world is just blank. When you fall into such a dark, secret place nothing in the world matters until later when you have to go home.

I pulled into my driveway around ten o'clock in the evening. I pushed the button for garage door and the large door opened, and I drove into the garage. I sat in the garage for several minutes shaking, I wasn't sure if I could even go inside the house. I was overcome with anxiety. Finally, I decided to just rest inside my locked truck for a while, until I felt like going inside. I closed the garage door and sat alone in the darkness and fell asleep.

Sometime in the early morning I woke up and decided it was time to face the inevitable. I had to go into the house. Inside the house, I surprisingly felt a sort of calming as I studied each piece of furniture and room decoration. Juliette had loved decorating our home, and I could see her personal touch everywhere I looked. For the first time in almost a year I tried to smile. We had a beautiful home; we had been so blessed.

The first day I was home I got cleaned up, shaved, and went for a haircut. After the haircut I headed to the bank to get my financial matters straightened out. After I returned home, I decided to sort through the piles of mail that had been delivered while I was away.

Many were bills that I had already taken care of, but then I found stacks and stacks of letters from Andrew addressed to Juliette and I, and stacks of letters from Andrew also addressed to you. I sat in the middle of the letters, and once again cried my eyes out. I assumed the letters had piled up in some military base, and they had delivered them after his death. What a cruel joke I thought; but still I was glad to get them.

I sorted the letters carefully putting your letters in one pile, and tying them together for you to read later, and ours in another stack. I slowly started reading the letters that Andrew had written to us. As I read the dates on each letter, I had chills run up my spine, because they were actually written after his death. It made no sense, because I had buried him months before the letters were even written.

I soon discovered that Andrew had been on a secret mission in Vietnam. He had become what was known as a 'Tunnel Rat.' The 'Tunnel Rats' were American, Australian, New Zealanders, and South Vietnamese soldiers who performed underground search and destroy missions during *the war. Most of the 'Tunnel Rats' were slimmer and smaller in stature than Andrew, but Andrew had been chosen because he was very* agile and *limber and could slither through the small tunnels easily. The tunnels were very narrow and confining.*

The underground tunnels were treacherous. The soldiers would enter a hole and come out 10 to 15 miles away. Being a 'Tunnel Rat' was one of the most dangerous jobs of the war. The pathways were narrow, and the passageways were pitch-black and extremely dangerous.

The tunnels were all dirt and rock and had been dug out by hand. Many of the tunnels had been dug during the war against the French in 1948. Communist's forces began digging a network of tunnels under the jungle terrain of South Vietnam in the late 1940s.

Most of the tunnels were hand and shovel dug, and they could only dig a short distance at a time. The small entrances to the tunnels were well-hidden and were covered with leaves. During the Vietnam War the tunnels were used by the Viet Cong soldiers as a hiding spot during combat, as well as serving as communication and supply routes, hospitals, food and weapons area and their living quarters for North Vietnamese fighters.

The Cu Chi tunnel systems led to underground ammunition stations, kitchens, air raid shelters and hospitals. The walls of the tunnels were often rigged with explosive traps. The soldiers that were selected were to crawl headfirst through the tunnels, armed with only a pistol, a knife, and a flashlight. They would then listen for any movement before moving forward. Some of the tunnels were 4 levels deep.

In the tunnels, the soldiers often found documents, pictures, ammunition, and crates full of heroin. Yet, as dangerous as the tunnels were most of the casualties were above ground. The soldiers that trained for 'Tunnel Rats' took a three-month course that covered mine detection, tunnel searching and demolitions.

During the Vietnam War the Viet Cong greatly exposed the network of tunnels which eventually covered a distance of 155 miles. The tunnels oftentimes had trip-wires, grenade mines, and boxes of live snakes or scorpions, and every few feet there were bats hanging from the walls.

In 1966, during the Vietnam War, the former North/South Vietnam border in the Vinh Linh District, started receiving more and more frequent bombings. As the attacks got heavier, the villagers finally moved their entire village underground. The entrance came in from the shoreline and it was heavily camouflaged by nature.

The underground city included all the needed accommodations, a hospital, a maternity ward, a series of water wells, toilets, ingenuously designed shafts for fresh air, and a venting kitchen for smoke that could not be detected in the air. The villagers had developed a secret knock so that they could tell the enemies from their own people.

At the peak of its existence, there were 600 villagers and soldiers living in the Vinh Moc tunnel village. 18 babies were born in the maternity ward and many still live in the area. No villagers lost their lives while living in the underground village during the bombings of the war.

Kathryn, once again I truly apologize to you for what I am about to tell you, but at the time, I felt it was the best thing to do. The normal procedure when a soldier dies in the jungle was to have his comrades prepare a grave wherever they happened to be. They would then wrap the corpse into the soldier's hammock, perform a short ceremony, and then just leave the body in the forest.

War is many horrible things, and one thing it is not is a careful bookkeeper. It wastes hundreds of lives, and in the deep jungle of Vietnam it was very difficult to keep track of all the soldiers who died. That is why 'The Tomb of the unknown soldier' in Washington D.C. was developed in the first place. Thousands of American dead soldiers are still missing in unmarked graves, they were either drowned, burned or just unaccounted for. The Tomb of the Unknown Soldier was first used on November 11, 1921, as a final resting place for one of America's unidentified World War I service members.

As confused as I was after reading all his letters, the only thing I knew for certain was, I had buried my son Andrew here in Arlington. We had a huge funeral. The body was badly destroyed and burned beyond recognition, and I had his dog tags with all his information on them. Andrew along with three other soldiers had been burned in a massive grave. All four soldiers had their dog tags on them, with their information when the bodies were sent home.

I still feel extremely nauseated, when I think about sitting in my front room, all alone that day reading letter after letter that Andrew had written to Juliette and me after I had buried both of them. Suddenly, it was as if God shouted out to me from heaven, and it suddenly became clear; WE HAD BURIED SOMEONE ELSES SON, not Andrew.

Kathryn, every single letter proved Andrew was alive. I didn't find out until after all these things had taken place, that every soldier in the Vietnam War had two sets of dog tags, one set was secretly attached to the inside of their boot strings, while the other was worn around their neck. I found after contacting the

United States Army that someone had been stealing the tags from the soldier's boots strings.

This was an evil, vicious war. There were so many disgraceful incidents that took place in Vietnam, that many of the Vietnam War soldiers will never talk about any of the things that had happened over there, once they returned home.

After sorting through records with the army, I discovered that Juliette and I were not the only parents who went through this hideous ordeal. After several months it was discovered that the three other soldiers in Andrew's unit were also sent home in flag-draped caskets. Their parents had also buried burned bodies they thought were their sons, and they too had endured the same horrific prank.

At the time, the four families were mourning the loss of their sons, Andrew and the other three soldiers were in special training, and they were not allowed to write home for several months. By the time Andrew could write home, we had already had a funeral, and Juliette had died, and I was gone to the mountains.

After several days of intense investigations through the war department, it was confirmed that Andrew was still alive, and we had actually buried the wrong person. By the time I finally caught up to where Andrew was now stationed, I was told that he had been wounded, and was sent to the USS Sanctuary a hospital ship where he had remained for 15 days, and then he was sent to San Francisco, California back in the states. San Francisco is where the army was sending wounded soldiers to rehabilitate. Andrew was eventually, sent to Texas to a burn facility. As soon as I got this information, I flew to Texas the following day to be with my son.

Andrew was at the Texas rehabilitation hospital for over 16 months. He was having a hard time learning to walk again, and he had trouble speaking for a short time. I stayed at the hospital for several weeks and I finally called your father's office. I acted very cordial as I ask him how you were doing. It was at that time that your father told me that you had met a young local doctor, and you were finally happy again, so I never told him about Andrew. Our conversation was short, and I doubt he even thought, anything about why I called.

At that time, Andrew was still struggling and I was not sure what his outcome would be. He was making progress, but I knew that your family had moved all the way across America to Idaho to start a new life. Our world here in Arlington had been so unsettled, and I felt it wasn't right to upset your plans too, so I decided not to contact you.

I saved the numerous letters that Andrew had written to you, and put them safely in a box, in the hall closet in case you would ever want to read them. I never opened them. By the time he was released from the hospital I assumed you would have already gotten married. I told Andrew, you had moved to Idaho and were married, and he could no longer reach you. That is why you never heard from him.

Again, sweet Kathryn I am so sorry for hiding all of this from you, but I knew it wasn't fair to upset your life with all the confusion of my family. With the 10 year-class-reunion coming up I did not want you to come to Arlington and discover for yourself, that

Andrew had survived the war, and you had never been told.

With much love,

Andrew Paul Brookshire II

Ten
Rejoice

After reading the letter, I looked at my mother and squealed, "He's Alive, My Andrew is alive." I quickly ran over to the phone and called Keith at work. I shouted in the phone, "Keith, Andrew is alive. I just got a letter from his dad. Start packing, we are going to the class reunion."

We sent back our acknowledgement papers, and within two weeks the twins and I, Keith, Keith's wife Margie, their little girl Beth, and my mom and dad were all loaded on a plane headed for Arlington, Massachusetts to the ten-year class reunion.

My parents were really excited to go to back to Massachusetts, because they had not been home since we moved to Idaho ten years earlier. I was so nervous I thought to myself, "Andrew has been through so much, what if he doesn't love me anymore. What if he has met someone else? What if he is married." So many troubling thoughts went through my head. His father had told me he was alive, but he didn't tell me anything else.

This is not at all how I had hoped our lives would be like. I had dreamed of his homecoming a thousand times, but I always visualized him coming home to me, not me flying three-thousand miles to find him.

We arrived at Arlington about 4:00 in the afternoon. Everyone for the reunion was staying at The Arlington Suites Hotel. It was a beautiful old landmark in the heart of Arlington. I had never been inside the huge hotel, but I had admired it from the outside since I was a little girl. Our family had driven past it, hundreds of times. My parents said they had once gone to a big fancy banquet there years ago, but they had never stayed in the hotel. We were all excited that this was the place where the reunion was going to take place.

Arlington was just as beautiful as we had remembered it. The huge old houses, the quaint quiet neighborhoods, the large beautiful tree-lined streets, it seemed like nothing had changed since the day we drove away and moved to Idaho ten long years earlier.

We went directly to our hotel. Many of the events would take place there. Keith and I and Margie had a formal dance party that evening in the ballroom downstairs in the hotel. It was the first event on the agenda.

Margie and I and my mom had gone shopping before we left Idaho, and we both found just the perfect dresses. Margie's dress was a red A-line scoop neck asymmetrical chiffon gown, that seemed to float as she walked. She looked beautiful in it.

I bought a dark green floor-length fitted gown, that had sparkling, intricate ornate beading, and a delicate matching wrap to place around my shoulders. I wore matching earrings, and matching spiked green heels. I felt like a princess, but my nerves were absolutely stressed out. I was like a young teenage adolescent High Schooler going to her first dance. I could not believe after everything that I have lived through, and after speaking in front of thousands of people, that seeing Andrew again had me so troubled.

It had been ten years, I had been married, had twin boys, and buried their father, but I couldn't believe how afraid I was. It was my Andrew, but we were very young when he went away, maybe after all these years he doesn't feel the same as he did. He has been through a lot too.

I kissed the boy's goodnight, they cuddled me and said, "Oh Mommy you look so beautiful, you look like a movie star." That was encouraging, and I needed it. I felt so insecure about everything. My mom stayed with the boys and Keith and Margie's little girl, and my dad walked me down to the ballroom. I wasn't quite brave enough to go to the dance alone.

We met Keith and Margie in the hall, then headed for the festivities. I felt like I might pass out, but I put one foot in front of the other and held on tightly to my father's arm. I really wanted to just turn around and go back up to the room.

We entered the beautifully decorated hall, and there were elegantly dressed couples standing everywhere around the room. There were also many people seated at several small tables, so the four of us walked over to an empty table and sat down.

One by one old friends came by our table to say hello. I slowly started feeling better after seeing so many familiar faces. Faces from my past that I thought I would never see again. We hugged, we talked, we laughed, we reminisced and I was really starting to enjoy myself. When the music started several couples got up to dance. Keith and Margie went out on the dance floor and I smiled at them, as I sat at the table with my dad.

Then suddenly I got a strange feeling that someone was watching me, I glanced around the room and I instantly saw Andrew. He was quietly standing with a bunch of our old classmates. It is amazing how you can spot one certain person, even if they are standing in the middle of a crowded room. They could be standing with a hundred people surrounding them, yet they are the only person that you see.

I shyly smiled at him as he slowly walked towards me. I am sure my heart stopped, and I could hardly breathe. I couldn't believe it. It really was my Andrew, and he was even more handsome than he was when we were younger. He timidly smiled at me, and put his hand out for me to dance with him. I felt like I was going to pass out, I was so overwhelmed, but somehow, I stood up and meekly walked towards him and tenderly melted into his arms.

They were playing the old songs from ten years ago. Tears ran down my face as I realized the song that was playing. They were playing 'Unchained Melody.' Andrew gently pulled me closer, and neither of us talked I just nuzzled my head into the bottom of his chin, just like I always did. I gradually relaxed, and I knew that this is where God planned for me to be. Praise the Lord my Andrew was back.

I found out later that Andrew's father had told him that he had sent me a letter. He also told him I was widowed and had twin boys. Andrew had never married; he told his dad that I was his forever love. I wish I would have known all of this before I came to Arlington; I wouldn't have been so terrified.

After the music was over, he walked me back to the table, and we both sat down. My dad politely talked to Andrew for a few minutes, and when my dad knew I was all right, he left and went back to the room to help my mom with all the kids. Everything seemed so unreal, it was as if the past ten years had never happened.

Keith, Andrew, and Margie and I laughed and told stories like none of us had ever been apart. It was like our lives were just on hold for a few years, and now it was time to start again. Of course, Andrew had never met Margie until tonight, but they just acted like they had known each other forever. There is nothing in this world as wonderful as getting together with old friends and reminiscing, laughing, and sharing the past.

Every time I looked over at Andrew, I realized he was staring at me and tenderly smiling. I do not think he could truly believe I was there. He held on tightly to my hand and lovingly played with my fingers all the time the four of us were talking. He was so attentive, and I think he was afraid to let go of me for fear I would disappear. I know because I had the same fears. Every time I looked into his eyes, I struggled to breathe, I just could not believe he was alive and sitting here with me. As many prayers that I had prayed, I still could not believe Andrew was real. I can never praise the Lord enough for allowing me to get my Andrew back.

When the dance was over, we all went back to my suite. Keith and Margie picked up their sleeping daughter, and went back to their room. My mother hugged Andrew and she talked to him for a few seconds, and then she too left for her room.

After they left, I went into check on the twins, and I suddenly realized that Andrew had followed me into to see the boys. He looked at my sons and smiled. As we walked back to the sitting room he lovingly said, “You have such handsome young men. What are their names? “

I looked down at the floor for a quick second and then sheepishly answered, “Sammy is named after his father, Samuel Dean,” and then I shyly looked directly into

Andrew's eyes and paused, before answering and I said, "Andy is Andrew Paul after my forever love."

With tears in his eyes, Andrew wrapped his arms around me and hugged me tenderly. Then I turned to look into his eyes, and I gently cupped his face in both of my hands and I lovingly kissed him for the first time in ten years. As we stood there, face to face we put are foreheads together and he gently sobbed, and with a humbling voice he whispered, "You named one of your sons after me?" He could barely talk, then he hugged me again, and slowly pulled a half of a heart necklace out from under his shirt. I had never seen the other half of the heart necklace before; it said: Kathryn Elizabeth Hartford is...

I took the wrap off from around my shoulders and I reached down inside my dress and pulled out my half of the heart necklace and looked directly into Andrew beautiful eyes and said, "I have never taken if off, since the night you gave it to me." We put the two hearts together and it read: Kathryn Elizabeth Hartford is...My Forever Love.

He held me tightly for several minutes and whispered in my ear, "I have loved you since I was thirteen years old, and I will love you until the day I am called to heaven. You will always be my forever love."

We talked for about an hour; and at 1:00 in the morning Andrew left. His suite was just up on the next floor, we kissed goodnight and we made plans to meet in the morning for breakfast. The twins always woke up around

6:30 each morning, so I knew it was going to be a short night, but I could not be happier. I closed my eyes and whispered, I Thessalonians 5:16-18. I knew that Andrew was on the floor above me saying the same verse. I closed my eyes and thanked the Lord saying, “Thank you Lord for bringing my Andrew back to me.”

At 8:00 the next morning the boys and I went down to the restaurant to meet Andrew, along with my parents, and Keith, and Margie and Beth. Andrew was already waiting at a large table by the time we arrived there for breakfast. He stood up and slightly kissed me on the cheek, and then hugged my mother and Margie hello. The twins had never seen Andrew before, and of course they had never seen anyone kiss their mommy before either. So, when I went to sit down next to Andrew, they both walked over to him and turned their face up to him, so that Andrew could kiss them on the cheek too.

Everyone laughed, but Andrew lovingly kissed each one of the twins, just as if it was the normal thing to do. I almost cried, “God is so good.” I was so worried about how I was going to introduce them, and the Lord took care of it.

Before sitting down, Andy asked Andrew, “What is your name?” Andrew smiled and looked over at me and said, “My name is Andrew.”

Andy candidly said, “Hey, my name is Andrew too.” Then he just innocently went over and sat next to his brother, and didn’t seem to think anything else about it.

When the check came Andrew had the waitress bring the check to him, and he just wrote his suite number on the ticket and handed it back to her. The waitress said, "Thank you Mr. Brookshire," and turned and walked away. It was strange because she acted like she knew him. Perhaps he ate there a lot.

After breakfast, we all drove into Boston to take the kids to the zoo and to have a nice lunch together downtown. Andrew and I acted as if we had never been apart. We laughed, we whispered, we talked; he treated me lovingly and respectfully, just like he always did. It was as if nothing had ever changed.

Although the boys had never seen Andrew before today, they treated him like he was part of our family, because that is how Uncle Keith, Aunt Margie, Beth, and their grandparents treated him. When we were at the zoo, Keith and Margie walked along each holding onto Beth's hands as she walked in between them.

Andrew and I were holding hands, and Andy walked up and grabbed Andrew by the hand, and Sammy grabbed my loose hand, and the four of us walked together through the zoo, just like a real family. My heart was filled with so much joy and happiness, I could not have felt more blessed.

I had my two beautiful boys, I had my beloved Andrew, and although I did not know what the Lord had planned for our future, I knew for today I could not stop praising his name, because everything was so perfect. The boys had just turned three years old, and they had never had a father.

Yet, it was so strange because they both acted like Andrew was who they would have chosen if they could choose a daddy, and I could tell Andrew was absolutely loving it. He hugged them, and talked to them just like he had been waiting for them all his life.

Later that afternoon, we all stopped for an ice cream cone. After every one had their cones, Andrew walked over and sat down on a bench, then Andy sat on one side of him, and Sammy sat on the other side. Andrew quickly looked up at me and slightly smiled, and kind of shrugged his shoulders. Before sitting down, I leaned over to him and kissed him to let him know everything was alright. When I went to sit down, my sons both grinned at me, and leaned up for me to kiss them too. Such a sweet feeling. I guess children really do learn a lot by watching both of their parents.

Around 3:00 in the afternoon we went back to the hotel to put the boys down for a rest. Andrew left for a short while to run some errands, so I took a few minutes to visit with my mom.

Around 6:00 that evening we had a catered dinner down in the common area on the grounds of the hotel. It was a beautiful outside event center. It had huge trees, shrubs, flowers, manicured grass sections, and rambling sidewalks that strolled in and around and throughout the large park area. The hotel suites encircled the grounds enclosing the park inside the hotel property. They had elegant tables scattered throughout the grounds for the reunion guest.

Everyone from the class reunion plus their families were invited. So, my parents and Keith, Margie and Beth and Andrew and I and the boys all went down to the park area. Even Andrew's dad came to the dinner to meet us. It was so nice seeing him again, he had been through so much in the past ten years, but he looked great. My dad and mom, and Andrew's dad hugged each other and instantly sat down and started reminiscing. They had been such good friends before Andrew went off to war. In fact, Juliette, Andrew's mom had ended up being one of my mom's best friends when we lived in Arlington.

The food was ready, and once again Sammy sat on one side of Andrew, and Andy sat on the other. So, I sat down on the other side of Sammy along with my parents and Keith, Margie, and Beth. We took lots of pictures; because we were truly a family.

Our class had lost a lot of classmates in Vietnam, but it was so great that so many of our other friends took the time to come to the reunion. Most of the people from our class had moved away from Arlington, but we soon discovered that Keith and I had traveled farther than anyone else in our class to get there. We were so glad that we came. The hotel was exquisite, the food was wonderful and of course, seeing my Andrew and all our old friends was an answer to my prayers. Everything seemed like a dream. I do not think I had ever been happier in my entire life.

After the dinner was over, all the people from the reunion loaded onto buses for an evening tour of some of the landmarks around Arlington. Arlington is the 350-year-old birthplace of Uncle Sam. It was the site of most of the fighting when the British marched through the area returning from the old North Bridge at the start of the Revolutionary War.

The town was originally named Menotomy, but the name was changed to Arlington in 1867 in honor of the heroes buried at Arlington National Cemetery in Arlington, Va. Uncle Sam was from Menotomy. Samuel Wilson was almost 9-years-old when the Battle of Menotomy took place. As an adult he started a meat-packing business in Troy, New York. That is where he became known as Uncle Sam. It was said that the U.S. stamped on the boxes of meat for the U.S. Army during the war of 1812, stood for Uncle Sam. The Arlington Historical District was listed on the U.S. National Register of Historic Places in 1974.

One of the most famous landmarks in Arlington is The Cyrus Dallin Museum. The museum had a special open house just for the people from our reunion, but as we walked through the museum, Sammy got sleepy, so Andrew just automatically picked him up and carried him everywhere we went. It wasn't long before Andy wanted to sleep too. It brought tears to my eyes when Andrew's father leaned over and picked Andy up, and put his head on his shoulder and carried him around, just like a normal grandpa would do. It was so surreal, every one of us acted like we had all been together forever.

As my mom and I walked behind Andrew and his dad, we both quietly moaned at the same time, and kind of giggled, then squeezed each other's hands because we could not believe that Andrew and his dad were so loving towards the twins. They treated them just like they have always been part of the family.

Love is such a strange emotion. It is something you cannot control. You cannot destroy it by running away. You cannot get over it by changing your life. You cannot forget it by being with someone else. Even death cannot erase it from your heart. To love someone is the most wonderful feeling you can ever experience. To sincerely love and be loved is the greatest blessing you can ever have.

After saying our good-nights, we all planned to meet the next morning to go to church with Andrew and his father at our old church. It is truly haunting to return to so many places from our childhood. Places that at one time had given us such an amazing life. Places that we had loved, and had never planned to leave. Wonderful places that we thought we would never see again.

As the taxi drove up to the church, I saw Andrew and his father waiting for us at the curb. I was in awe of how great the old church looked. It was such a beautiful old building with the massive stained-glass windows and huge carved wooden doors. This church held so many memories for our family. My parents were married here, and Keith and I had been dedicated, and baptized in this church. This was the church where I had first met Andrew so many years ago.

When we walked through the huge doors, we instantly saw rows and rows of familiar faces. My mother and Father saw old friends that they had known for over 30 years.

Many of our classmates that were in town for the class reunion walked in behind us. They too had once belonged to our church youth group, and had also gone there for most of their childhood.

It was like walking back in time. Nothing had changed; there were rows and rows of padded pews, with large elegant chandeliers precisely hung throughout the massive hall. I marveled at the familiar curved high ceilings and the huge marble pillars that held up the beautiful upstairs balcony. The exquisitely painted arched windows literally took my breath away, although they had always been there, it was like seeing them for the first time. And the giant carved wooden cross displayed behind the choir was something I had always cherished.

As I looked around, I noticed the entire church was packed, many faces I had never seen before, but everyone was smiling and nodding their heads hello. I had always loved this church. It was such a huge part of my life. I felt like I was home.

Before the service started a man that I did not recognize, stood up in front of the church and ask all the of people who had come to Arlington for the class reunion to please stand, so they could welcome us. Around forty or fifty people and their families stood up around the sanctuary and everyone clapped.

Then the man up front said, “Of course, even our own Pastor, Pastor Andrew is a part of this reunion so one of our Associate Pastors, Pastor Loren will be giving the message today, but Pastor Andrew has a special surprise for us at the end of the service.”

I quickly looked at Andrew and whispered, “You are the minister here?”

He put his arm around my shoulder and pulled me tight, and kissed the top of my forehead, and smiled and continued to look straight ahead.

“Andrew became a minister?” My thoughts whirled inside my head, “He always wanted to be a minister, that is what we had planned, and I was going to be a minister’s wife.”

I do not think I heard a word that Pastor Loren said, because so many thoughts were spinning through my mind. While I was back in Idaho mourning the loss of Andrew, graduating from college, becoming a nurse, getting married, burying my husband, having the twins, and speaking before huge conferences; Andrew was here putting his life in order just like we had planned.

I was not sure what to think, so much had changed in the past ten years. Yet, as I looked around the church it was uncanny; because so much had stayed the same. I silently thought, “Can a person really go back and start again where they left off?” My mind was so confused. The past few days had been a dream-come-true, but I guess I was saddened to discover Andrew had done so much with his life without me. If only I had known that he had lived through the war, things would have been different. Of course, I wouldn't have Andy and Sammy. I slowly shook my head trying to clear my confusion, and once again I tried to hear the end of the sermon.

I suddenly realized that Andrew was getting out of his seat and heading up towards the front of the church. He went to the stage and picked up his guitar and then he smiled at me, and asked me through the microphone to come forward and sing with him.

Although, I had spent the past few years performing in front of huge audiences, I felt nervous. As I cautiously walked up to the piano, everyone in the church was clapping and encouraging me to go up on stage. Suddenly, I heard Andrew introducing me to his congregation. He said, "For those of you that don't know this beautiful lady, this is my forever love, Kathryn Elizabeth." He was absolutely beaming as he talked, she doesn't know it yet, but I am hoping she will do a special song with me this morning. He laughed and said, "We haven't practiced this in ten years, but we had performed it so many times when we were in High School that I'm sure Kathryn will remember it." He looked over at me and said, "In case you need music, it is on the piano." Without taking his eyes off me, he told the audience, "We sang this song together when we were in High School because Elvis Presley was popular, and he performed it on stage several times. This is truly our life's song, *How Great Thou Art*."

As soon as Andrew started to sing in his deep tenor voice, my heart rejoiced, and I instantly remembered the many times we had performed this song together. I felt such peace. I knew this is exactly where the Lord had planned for me to be. Singing with Andrew had always been the joy of my life, and I quickly realized that nothing had really changed.

After we sang, I stayed at the piano, and Andrew did the closing prayer for the congregation. He had such a powerful voice. I was in awe, and I knew he was still my same Andrew.

After the service was over, Andrew reached for my hand and led me to the back of the church with him so we could greet each church member as they walked by, on their way out the doors. I Was told that this is something he did each Sunday, but this time it was different, he had me standing by his side.

Member after member hugged me and welcomed me home. They all knew that I was coming to Arlington, because Andrew had told them. Even new people in the church that I had never met before, were anxious to meet me because they had heard so much about me.

One person after another told me how wonderful Andrew was. I could tell that the congregation just loved him, but even in High School he was a fabulous speaker. I soon discovered that he had taken over as the head pastor three years ago. The year when I was burying Samuel and delivering the twins. He had been ordained when he was only 25 years old. I was told that he started studying to be a minister right after he got out of the hospital after he was wounded in Vietnam. Andrew had always seemed more mature than other young men his age. That is what attracted me to him in the first place, so many years ago when we were only in the 8th grade.

I was told that he took a correspondence course from home and he got his bachelor's degree in Christian studies with an emphasis on worship and leadership. He started out by being the music leader, and he was the music leader while he was completing his courses. The military had special benefits for military veterans.

When we attended this church ten years ago Pastor Bill Jamison was the minister and he had been at the church for over fifteen years. He was the minister that did the funeral, when they thought Andrew had been killed. He also did the funeral for Johnny Johnson, and several other local boys killed in Vietnam, but after his son Mark was killed, he went on leave and never came back. I was told that many of the regular church members left at that time too. They had several interim pastors while they waited for Andrew to finish school. One lady told me that the church had nearly doubled since Andrew took over as the head Pastor.

When I looked at Andrew, I was amazed; because he had accomplished everything that he had intended to do with his life. Even after all these years, he was incredible. I watched him as he greeted member after member as they walked by, and I could tell that he honestly loved each and every one of them.

He was unbelievable. It was like watching a celebrity. He was handsome, self-confident, and intelligent and everybody seemed to greatly admire him. I felt like I was in a dream. Andrew seemed so happy and content at being the head Pastor of this gigantic congregation. I could not help but fall in love with him all over again. It was mind-boggling; I just couldn't stop staring at him. I always knew he was impeccable, but today I realized that now that he is older, everyone else knows how perfect he is too.

It wasn't until later that day that I was told that Andrew had privately called my father a short time before we came to Arlington, but they never told anyone. After Andrew discovered that his dad had written me a letter, and that I had signed up for the reunion, he called my father at his office in Idaho to ask him some questions about me. Andrew's father had given him the number where he could reach my father. After they talked, they decided it was best to let things work out the way they needed to go, and not tell anyone until later that they had talked to each other on the phone.

Apparently, Andrew was just as worried about seeing me after ten years, as I was about seeing him. So much had gone on in both of our lives since we were last together, and he had the same fears that I had. My father told him that our family was informed that he had been killed in

Vietnam, and that I needed to move on with my life, so that is what I was forced to do.

He told him that I never dated anyone for several years until I met Dr. Samuel Peterson. I was not looking for anyone, but the doctor was one of my teachers and after the class was completed, he invited me out to lunch. He told him that Samuel was several years older than I was, and that I would have never married him if I had known Andrew was still alive. He reminded Andrew several times that I had never changed my feelings towards him; I always considered him my forever love.

My father told Andrew that our entire family had relentlessly mourned his death when we thought he had been killed in Vietnam. He told him the only reason that I had gotten married was because we thought Andrew was never coming back. My dad also told him that I had dated Samuel for a year and a half before we got married, and then we were only married a little over a year when he decided to leave for Africa with doctors without borders. He told him that I had planned to go to Africa with Sam, but I found out I was pregnant, and I was not allowed to go.

He said, "Samuel was gone for several months when he contacted Malaria and died." He then told him, "Samuel was a wonderful Christian man, and he came from a well-known Idaho family." He told him, "The twin's father had died two months before the boys were even born, so they had never even known their father. Kathryn has raised the boys alone, with the help of both families, and she is very close with Samuel's parents."

He told Andrew that I got my nursing degree, but after Samuel died, I did not go back into nursing, I had become a conference speaker, and I had been singing and speaking in front of huge audiences for the past few years. That is when Andrew got the idea to have me sing with him on stage. My father also told him that I still wore 'My Forever Love' necklace and chain, so Andrew knew I still loved him.

My father had encouraged Andrew enough that Andrew told his whole congregation that I was coming back to Arlington. He said, "I have prayed and prayed about it, and the Lord has given me peace." That is why everyone was so anxious to meet me.

Keith, Margie, and Beth flew back to Idaho on Tuesday, but my mom, dad and the twins and I planned to stay in Arlington for a while. My dad wanted to visit the people at his former company in Boston, and my mom wanted to look up her old friends. Dad had always loved his job there, and he missed many of his people.

The twins and I spent every waking hour with Andrew. We visited Legoland Discovery Center, Martin's Park, and playground, we went to Princess Day at the zoo, we visited Boston Children's Museum, the New England Aquarium, and we rode the Swan Boat ride in the public gardens.

Each day was packed with family outings. We rode the 60-minute Historical Sightseeing Cruise, we went through the wonderful Museum of Science, we rode the trolley, and we shopped at every toy store. We even walked the Old Freedom Trail and of course, we spent time at the church every time the doors were open.

Sammy and Andy adored Andrew; you could tell that they loved having a 'Daddy' around. It was so fun going places as a family. Andrew was so good with the boys; people treated him like he was their true father, and I could tell he unquestionably loved every minute with them. He acted like God had sent them to me, just for him... and maybe God did.

Some nights we would put the boys to bed, and my mom and dad would stay with them while we had a late-night supper in a nice restaurant. We would sit and visit and reminisce and talk about our future. We knew our future held some big changes for our entire family, including Samuels's family back in Idaho. I sincerely loved Samuel's family and they had been by my side all through Samuel's time in Africa, his death, his funeral and of course in helping with the twins, and I knew that if I stayed in Arlington they would be devastated.

So, Andrew and I prayed together, "Dear Lord, please guide us in your wisdom. We know that you have skillfully brought us back together according to your divine plan for our lives. Please guide us in the path that is right."

I called Samuel's mother the next day and before I could say anything she said, "We love you Kathryn, and we love our grandsons, but your mother and father had the boys call us yesterday, just to talk." She quietly told me, "We could tell the boys absolutely idolize Andrew; they talked a mile a minute about all the fun things you had been doing together. They said they had always wanted a daddy because they had never had one." She continued, "They said Andrew was a minister in a beautiful, huge church and they wanted to live in Arlington with Andrew and to be a real family."

She tearfully told me, "Kathryn, we know that Andrew was the love of your life. Samuel knew that long before he ever married you, but still you were a true devoted wife to Samuel, and you gave us two beautiful boys, and we are so thankful for that." She continued, "Melvin and I have talked it over and after shedding many tears we want you to know that you have our blessings." She continued, "Grandpa and I will just have to take a trip out to Massachusetts at least once a year, to come and see our extended family."

I got off the phone and just sat there in disbelief. When Andrew walked in the room, I ran to him and wrapped my arms around his neck and sobbed into his shoulder and said, "They gave us their blessings."

Eleven

Give Thanks

Andrew's Sunday morning message was a little bit shorter than it usually was, and at the close of the service Andrew asked the twins and me to come up on stage. Then he got down on one knee and in front of his entire congregation, he asked all three of us to marry him and be a family.

The whole congregation cheered in approval. Andrew then opened a small box that held a beautiful diamond wedding set, it was the most gorgeous wedding ring I had ever seen. He smiled as he slipped the ring on my finger and whispered, "This set had belonged to my mother, and my father said she would want you to have it." He then gave each of the boys a solid gold cross to wear around their necks to show that he was marrying all three of us.

As Andrew was doing the closing prayer for the church service, I closed my eyes and silently said inside my head; 1 Thessalonians 5: 16-18, Rejoice always, pray continuously, give thanks in all circumstances; for this is God's will for you in Christ Jesus. When I opened my eyes, I saw a man walk up to the stage with two giant flower bouquets that he placed on each side of the platform.

Suddenly a distinguished friend from our past, our old minister, Pastor Bill Jamison stepped up from the front row and came up on the stage. He walked over and hugged me, and then he went to the microphone and proudly said, "I was asked to come and perform a wedding here this morning for a special couple that I have known since they were teenagers."

Andrew had organized everything for our wedding. He wanted to have the wedding before my mom and dad had to fly back to Boise. A man named Byron Reynolds, from the clerk's office was a member in our congregation, and he had the marriage license ready for us to sign after the ceremony was completed.

Andrew's dad and my parents came up on the stage to stand with us. My mom proudly placed a flowered veil on my head, and then handed me a beautiful wedding bouquet and took her place as my Matron-of-Honor. Andrew's dad, my dad, and Andy and Sammy proudly stood up with Andrew. A man with a camera came up and began taking impromptu pictures.

I was in shock, and as I looked out over the congregation; I realized that we were really having a wedding. I joyfully smiled at the congregation and thought to myself, "We have more people at this wedding than Samuel and I did at our huge wedding in Idaho, and my mother and I had planned the Idaho wedding for months."

Everything was perfect, except that Keith and Margie and other family members were not here for this extraordinary occasion. Yet, I had waited 15 years for my true love and I was more than ready to become his wife.

Apparently, Andrew and my parents had arranged for us to have a huge reception next month back in Idaho so that Keith, Margie and Beth, and Samuel's family would be there to help us celebrate our marriage.

Pastor Jamison started the ceremony with our memory verse: 1 Thessalonians 5:16-18, Rejoice always, pray continually, give thanks in all circumstances; for this is God's will for you in Christ Jesus. Within twenty minutes I had become Mrs. Andrew Brookshire. I could not have planned a more picture-perfect wedding if I had planned it myself. When Pastor Jamison concluded the ceremony, he read the verse: Ecclesiastes 3:11 it said, "He has made everything beautiful in His time."

He then told us to turn around and he introduced us to 'OUR' congregation. He said, "May I now introduced to you, Pastor, and Mrs. Andrew Brookshire the 3rd." The entire congregation stood up and clapped and cheered, and the giant church bells in the steeple above our heads, began to ring announcing to the world that I had married my forever love.

Then Pastor Loren, the associate pastor announced, "The ladies of the church have prepared a luncheon celebration for the entire congregation. They also have a beautiful wedding cake that was made and designed by our own professional wedding cake creator and church member, Georgia Scott. Everything will be served in the reception hall. Please come help us celebrate the long-awaited marriage of our pastor and his wife, Kathryn Elizabeth."

I found out later, that most of the people in the congregation knew that we were having a surprise wedding that day. People came from miles around just to be there for our wedding. Even the balconies of the church were full. My parents were told, and of course Andrew's father knew, in fact, it seemed everyone knew about the wedding, except for the twins and I.

Andrew and I had already talked about living in the church parsonage after we were married, that is where he has been living for the past three years. It was a beautiful old, four-bedroom house that was located directly behind the church. It had a lot of possibilities, and I was excited to make it our family home. It had been remodeled over the years and it was a striking Arlington residence. My mom told me she would help me decorate it before she went back to Idaho.

We could put up new drapes and buy a few new chairs. I was not sure what to do with all my furniture in Idaho, but we had accomplished so many hurdles already I had faith we could work out those obstacles too. After all, in the past few weeks we have adjusted to being back together, having two boys, getting engaged, having a wedding, deciding on a home in Arlington, so I know everything else will also fall into place. It seems like things have happened so fast, yet most of our plans were made ten years ago, and it has taken ten years to put them together.

My mom and dad took care of the boys for a couple of days, so that Andrew and I could have some time to ourselves, and have a short honeymoon. Andrew had arranged for the honeymoon suite at The Arlington Suites Hotel. It is the hotel where the reunion had been held, and I knew the room would be extravagant, because the entire hotel was magnificent.

The hotel had ornate black marble walls that surrounded the entrance as you entered the building, and the massive high ceilings were several stories high above the huge lobby area. A number of exquisite crystal chandeliers hung elegantly throughout the chamber, and the sophisticated lobby had large white overstuffed high-back chairs, beautifully carved tables, with fresh flower arrangements placed around the entire lobby, and a giant stone fireplace covering one whole wall.

The beautiful old hotel was an ideal place for our first night as husband and wife because it was elegant, yet familiar. Andrew was so thoughtful, and he knew me so well, even after we have been apart for so long, he remembered every detail of what I might want.

I cherished my Andrew so much, and I loved my beautiful wedding ring set. I could not stop staring at it. It meant even more to me because it had belonged to my dearest friend, Juliette, Andrew's mother. I knew it was extremely expensive and yet Andrew and his father had given them to me. This entire day was just a magnificent romantic fantasy, but if it was a dream, I sure did not want to wake up. God is so good. He has given me so much.

When we got to the hotel, we ordered a candlelight dinner to be delivered to our room. The room was the entire top floor of the right wing of the hotel. I don't think I have ever been in such a royal atmosphere before, and I have been in a lot of beautiful hotels. It was an absolute fairytale suite. It was gorgeous with a huge balcony looking out over the entire town of Arlington.

Arlington had so many trees, it was charming, quaint and I was so delighted to be back here once again. We had finished eating dinner out on the balcony, and we were sitting in the deck chairs looking out over the city, and I closed my eyes and thought to myself, "Everything that has happened to me in my lifetime has brought me to this point. My life has gone full circle to bring me back to Andrew and to Arlington."

Suddenly Andrew seemed very nervous, he kind of paced back and forth across the balcony a few times, and I just sat quietly and watched him. I had noticed that he barely touched his prime rib dinner, but everything else had been so perfect I just dismissed it, but now I realized something was terribly wrong. He wiped his hands across his face and then through his hair and bowed his head for a few seconds and then looked directly into my eyes and said, "I have something I need to tell you, and I didn't want to tell you until after we were married."

I instantly felt sick, and I could hardly catch my breath. I sat back in my chair and stared directly into his face and I thought, "What was he waiting to tell me." I was so scared, I felt like my world was once again going to crumble right before my eyes.

As I watched him, I could not believe how good-looking he was, he looked just like the movie star Ricky Nelson, with his serious, unassuming pouty lips and his humble charisma, but as handsome as he was, he seemed so disturbed that I thought I might cry. He was only a few inches from my face as he leaned forward even closer, and he held on tightly to my hands and I could tell he was quivering, he was terribly disturbed. I was so frightened of what he was going to say, I did not know if I could handle it or not.

He was so serious as he said, "Kathryn, I have not been entirely truthful with you." My heart sank as he continued, "I am not only a minister; my dad and I own this hotel. It had belonged to my grandfather Andrew Paul Brookshire Senior, and he passed away two years ago and my dad and I were his only heirs. My father and I have wonderful people that run the hotel for us, so we don't actually work here." He was still apologetic as he explained, "That is why the committee had the class reunion here."

I couldn't help it, I burst out laughing. I wrapped my arms around his neck and continued to giggle, "Oh my sweet

Andrew, I thought you were going to tell me something terrible, and believe me, I have had a lot of terrible news in my lifetime, and that is not terrible news. Why would you be afraid to tell me?"

I was so relieved; I could not stop hugging him and kissing him. My sweet, sweet Andrew, he was afraid to tell me he was wealthy. With so many life changes for the twins and I in the past few weeks, Andrew being wealthy was one of the easiest things to accept. I felt such relief, I kissed him over and over again and said, "Oh my sweet husband, I loved you when you were a young teenager, I loved you in High school, I loved you when you went away to war and I love you today rich or poor."

He hugged me tighter and tighter and whispered in my ear, "Oh Kathryn, I am so relieved. I was afraid you would feel different about me if you knew I was wealthy, that is why I was afraid to tell you before the wedding."

He immediately felt starved, and went back to the table to finish his dinner. I couldn't help but shake my head back and forth in amazement as I watched him relax and eat his prime rib. I silently thought as tears streamed down my face, "He truly is honorable and flawless. He has always been my brave courageous warrior. Thank you, Jesus, but how could someone who has accomplished so much in his lifetime still be so humble?"

Our room had a hot tub so after dinner we decided to sit in the hot tub for a while. This was the first time I had seen Andrew with his shirt off since he was in Vietnam. He had massive disturbing scars all over his body that you could not see when he was fully dressed.

He told me, “1968 was probably the worst year of the war. That is the year we all left for Vietnam, right after graduation. The Tet Offensive was a coordinated series of North Vietnamese attacks on more than 100 cities and small towns in South Vietnam by North Vietnamese and Viet Cong forces. Ending with an estimated 33,000 enemy casualties, and 3,500 allied casualties, a third were Americans. Nearly half of 12,000 wounded were Americans.”

“Actually, countless people called it the turning point in the war.” He solemnly continued, “Our unit was hit by white phosphorus grenades several different times. Many of my friends were killed instantly. I saw horrible things in Vietnam, young men hobbling around with their arms and legs blown off.”

He covered his face with his hands and thought about it for a few seconds and then continued, “Many of the guys had no faces, big strong men were screaming and pleading to God and falling to the ground in pain. So many of the soldiers looked like young boys that should have been home going to their High School prom.”

He shook his head back and forth then put his face in his hands again as he reminisced of that hideous time, “When my unit was hit, I played dead and I lay silent surrounded by the dead bodies and that is why I survived. After I was rescued, I spent months in the hospital and they would immerse us in big tanks to remove the damaged skin. It was so horrifying, and I could hear other injured soldiers screaming in pain up and down the hospital halls. They lost ears, eyes, arms and legs or half of their face." He said, "I was in the hospital for months. Many of the guys that were in the hospital with me did not survive." He closed his eyes and shook his head, "They couldn't tolerate the pain. I was one of the lucky ones."

I wrapped my arms around my husband, and told him how much I loved him just as he was. I smiled and said, "I love the person inside the scars, the person that has been my love since I was thirteen years old. You are so kind, so thoughtful, so brilliant, so handsome, so humble, and you are my husband."

I smiled and looked at my left hand and studied my beautiful rings and proudly stated, "I am Mrs. Andrew Brookshire the 3rd and I couldn't be happier." I put my face close to his face and whispered, "To me you are perfect."

Shortly before my parents left to go back to Idaho my dad handed me a letter; it was the letter that Andrew had written to my father ten years earlier as he was leaving for Vietnam. Andrew had given it to me to give to my father. I had given it to my dad right away, but this is the first time I had read it. I had forgotten all about it. My father had read it and hid it away so that he could share it with me when Andrew returned from Vietnam. Of course, Andrew never returned so I never saw it until now.

The letter read:

Dear Mr. Hartford,

Today I am leaving for the Vietnam War to do my duty for my country. When I return from Vietnam, I would ask your permission to marry your daughter Kathryn Elizabeth. I know that Kathryn is my Christian soul-mate. God showed me this in a vision when I was only thirteen years old, and I have waited for His divine timing to make her my wife. I have loved her since we were in the Junior High youth group, and I promise to love her until the day God calls us home.

Waiting for God's perfect time,

Your future son-in-law Andrew Paul Brookshire the 3rd

After I read the letter, I covered my face in disbelief, because I had never told anyone about my dreams of marrying Andrew. Fifteen years later I am now finding out that the Lord gave him the same dream.

Twelve

Pray Continuously

Our marriage was a true love story. Although, I had first been married to Samuel, my life with Andrew was much different. I felt complete, everything just seemed right this time. I loved being a minister's wife, and my boys loved having a father, and I was amazed at how willingly the ladies of the church accepted me into the flock. One of the reasons that everyone admired Andrew so much was because he firmly believed that 'Jesus is the real Pastor of the church.' The meaning of the word Pastor means shepherd, and the Lord God is the ultimate shepherd.

Shortly after my mother left for Idaho, several ladies from the church came by to help me get settled into the church parsonage. The parsonage was a beautiful old stone home that we could live comfortably in for many years. Because all my personal property like dishes, pans, and silverware, was three thousand miles away in Idaho, we went shopping to purchase things to set up my new family household. The ladies were such a help to me.

Within a few days, I discovered that Pastor Loren's wife Jeanne, would soon become one of my very best friends. Jeanne had two small children; Jimmy was a year younger than the twins, and their daughter Ellen was two years older. Having a close friend made my move back to Arlington so much easier. I knew I would not be quite as homesick for my family in Idaho if I had someone I could trust and feel close to. I was 28 years old and I had never lived away from my mom and dad before, they had always been there to help me with whatever I needed.

A month after our wedding, the four of us flew back to Idaho to see family and to attend the beautiful reception my mother and Samuel's mother had put together for us. I was anxious to show 'My Andrew' off to all my Idaho friends. Most everyone I had met when I moved to Idaho had heard of Andrew, but they had all been told that he had been killed in Vietnam when I met Samuel.

It was wonderful seeing friends again, but I knew that my life now belonged in Arlington. We hired a rental agency and rented out my Boise house, and before leaving Andrew promised my family that he would send me home to visit Idaho, at least once a year.

He also let everyone know that we would have a place for anyone to stay if they wanted to come and visit us in Massachusetts. They were welcome at our house, but he told them, "We can also always find you a room at The Arlington Suites Hotel."

We stayed in Boise for two whole weeks, and as we got on the plane to fly back to Arlington, my feelings were bitter sweet, because this time I knew this was a true goodbye. It was time to seriously begin a new chapter in my life.

Being a minister's wife was very hectic. We were always busy. Our church had a Christian Preschool so the boys went to preschool two mornings a week. There were endless outreach programs, along with missionary work, a large choir, multiple lady's groups, men's, and women's Bible studies, and of course Sunday mornings, Sunday evenings, and Wednesday evening church. Every Tuesday morning at 7:00 A.M., Jeanne and I would meet for coffee and prayer time together. She was such a strong Christian support in my life.

Before long, I was asked to speak at numerous events, and I often led many of the lady's groups. With a congregation this size there were many people in need, and Andrew and I visited people in the hospital at least twice a week while the boys were in preschool. Our world was extremely demanding, but we all loved our new lives.

We had been married several months when one of the older couples in our church, Glenn, and Helen Simpson, dropped by the house late one evening. The couple had received tragic news about their daughter and her family. Apparently, their daughter, son-in-law and three children had been mysteriously murdered in a strange murder-suicide event in Guyana where they had been living.

Helen was unable to travel, but Glenn asked Andrew if he would go with him and his friend, Dr. Dwayne Watson to help identify the bodies. His friend, Dr. Watson was one of our church elders. He wanted Dr. Watson and Andrew to go with him because Andrew was his pastor, and Dwayne Watson was a retired doctor and he would be a big help in identifying the bodies. As horrible as the situation appeared, Andrew knew he could not let Glenn and Dr. Watson go to Guyana alone so he agreed to go with them.

The Simpsons and the Watsons had been members of our church congregation for over thirty years. Andrew had met the daughter, Gretchen and her husband, Bill when he first came back to Arlington after getting released from the hospital after Vietnam. As terrifying as everything appeared, Andrew felt he needed to support Glenn and Helen.

Their daughter, Gretchen was Glenn and Helen's only child, so the three grandchildren were their only grandchildren, and they had lost them all. As nauseating as the trip would be, Andrew new he must go to help the family.

The entire situation was so horrifying because they were told that there were hundreds of dead bodies involved in the murder-suicide. There was a national emergency declared, and the airlines offered a special low-price fare for people to fly to Guyana to identify the victims.

Andrew and the other two men boarded a plane the very next morning to travel to Jonestown, 2,900 miles away. The families were told to go to Jonestown immediately because the tropical heat would quickly decompose the bodies and they would be harder to recognize. Every one of the families were warned that their relatives were just lying around outside on the grounds of the property, and they did not know what to do with all 909 bodies in the tropical heat.

Even after all the warnings, when the men arrived in Guyana, they were still shocked to see the hundreds and hundreds of dead bodies covering the large area they called the People's Temple. The men were absolutely sickened as they saw bodies piled everywhere they looked.

The three men would later discover that Jonestown, Guyana would go down in history as one of the most harrowing tragedies in American history. On November 18, 1978 cult leader Jim Jones of the People's Temple died along with 909 members of his congregation. Every one of the members died from apparent cyanide poisoning in a 'revolutionary suicide.' At least 304 of the dead bodies were those of young children.

Authorities did not know what to do with all the bodies, they couldn't just bury them in a mass grave. That is why they decided to have family members come from all over the world to claim their relatives before they were completely unrecognizable.

The original temple was started in Indianapolis, but by the late 1970's Jim Jones had three churches in California. After moving the church to San Francisco in 1971, his church was increasingly accused of financial fraud, physical abuse, and mistreatment of children. He also had many older senior citizens that lived in the People's Temple, and they just handed over their social security checks to Jones. After several lawsuits, the paranoid leader then moved his entire temple out of California to Guyana to build a socialist utopia in Jonestown, Guyana.

There was a California Congressman named Leo Ryan that had been a High School teacher, and he also had a friend whose granddaughter was a member at Jonestown and they were very concerned about her and her family.

A group of former temple members and concerned relatives of the current members convinced Congressman Leo Ryan to investigate the settlement in person. Apparently, Ryan's district included constituents both among the relatives of the members, and among some of the people who were now actually living in in Jonestown itself.

Congressman Ryan arrived at Jonestown, Guyana with a group of journalists on November 17th, and at first the visit went well. But the next day, on November 18th, as Congressman Ryan and the other delegates were about to leave things changed. Several of the People's Temple residents approached Congressmen Ryan and his group, and asked if they could leave with them. They wanted to get out of Guyana.

Jones became distressed at the defection of his followers and he ordered one of his lieutenants to attack Congressman Ryan with a knife. Congressman Leo Ryan escaped from that incident unharmed, but Jones then ordered his companions to ambush and kill the group as they attempted to leave. The congressman and four others were murdered as they boarded their chartered planes at the nearby airstrip.

Richard Dwyer was deputy chief of mission at the U.S. embassy in Guyana. He was among those boarding the planes to leave. Dwyer survived by laying perfectly still after he had been shot. They thought he was dead. Richard Dwyer is how they later learned of all the harrowing events of the Jonestown Massacre.

After the killings at the airstrip Jones then commanded everyone in his group to gather at the main pavilion. According to later reports, the youngest members were the first to die. We discovered that Glenn's young grandchildren were given syringes with a mixture of cyanide sedatives, and poisoned grape juice, similar to Kool-Aid. The parents used syringes to put the mixture into their own children's throats. Adults then drank the concoction while guards surrounded the pavilion. It was discovered that the mass-suicide was carried out because of the murders at the airstrip a few hours earlier that day.

The Jonestown Massacre would go down in history as the largest mass suicide in modern history, and resulted in the largest single loss of American life in a non-natural disaster. A tape made by Jim Jones was discovered with him talking to his people the last 45 minutes of their lives, he was telling the people to kill themselves.

Andrew, Glenn, and Dr. Watson spent hours walking through masses of lifeless bodies before they came upon the remains of Glenn's daughter and her family. There was no rhyme or reason to the location of any families. His daughter and her family had died all together in one place, so once they discovered the bodies, they found all five of them.

After the families identified the remains, the bodies were loaded into waterproof canvas body bags, and coffin-like metal transport containers. U.S. military helicopters shuttled the dead out of the deep jungle so that they could be sent home to their own home state. Most of the bodies were claimed, but the 400 unclaimed remains were sent to California, and they were buried in the Evergreen Cemetery in Oakland, California.

Andrew, Glenn, and Dr. Watson returned home, and within a few days the bodies arrived. Of course, Andrew was asked to officiate the funeral of all five members of Glenn and Helen Simpson's young family. The funerals were held the week of the Thanksgiving holiday.

This was probably one of the hardest things Andrew ever had to do as head Pastor of the church. It was such an overwhelming experience that he had nightmares for days after going to Jonestown.

A short time after the funerals, we lost Glenn's wife Helen. She had not been well for a few months and losing her entire family was more than she could bear. A few days after her funeral Glenn was found sitting alone in his front room. He had overdosed on the sleeping medicine the doctor had given him to sleep.

Glenn and Helen Simpson were only 63 years old. This whole nightmare was just too much for the couple to endure. In a matter of days, Andrew was forced to perform seven funerals for the Simpson family. Even as strong as Andrew was, the entire situation was just too intolerable for him to get through.

The church board and the church elders were very aware of everything Andrew had been forced to undergo. We had such caring church members, and the head of the church board came to Andrew and told him, "This has been a horrendous situation for you to deal with." He continued, "The board feels you need to take your family away for a while and rest. Take a vacation; Go play with your kids and see some new scenery." He said, "A person can only handle just so much, and this has been much more than anyone should have to endure. He handed Andrew a check from the church so that we could take our kids away and rest."

I remembered how much the trip across America had helped me after Andrew left for Vietnam. So, the next morning, the church rented us a small motorhome, and we loaded it up with everything the boys would need, clothes, food, toys, all essentials, and we headed South for a journey to see some of God's country. With such short notice, we decided we could just buy whatever else we needed along the way. We didn't have time to plan anything out, and Andrew was in no frame of mind to plan out a lengthy vacation anyway. We needed to just go, and get away. It was the end of November so we headed south to avoid bad weather.

None of us had ever traveled in a motorhome before, but Andrew and I both felt like this would be a better change for us than flying off somewhere. The motorhome was small enough that I could help drive, if need be. The twins had never taken a road trip and they were in awe of everything they saw. The fields, the farmland, the cows, the rivers, the high mountains, and the wide-open spaces. They marveled at the big trucks, the shiny cars, and the fast noisy motorcycles, and Andrew appreciated seeing everything through the innocent eyes of his boys.

We saw the beautiful white sandy beaches of New Jersey, then on towards Virginia to tour the Skyline Shenandoah National Park. I cherished the time of coziness with just the four of us huddled together inside the small motorhome. We laughed, we talked, we saw places we could have never seen while flying in an airplane. We bought delicious double-scoop ice cream cones at the local ice cream parlor, the boys loved ice cream, but there was no way they could ever eat that much ice cream, but we bought them for them anyway. We threw rocks in the cold mountain stream, we saw a skunk, three foxes, several racoons, soaring eagles, deer, hawks, and even one small black bear. This was truly a trip of family bonding for all of us, and each day I could see the tenseness disappear from Andrew's shoulders.

We could sit inside the motorhome and play games, or watch Television or take naps. If we were near a town, we could get all dressed up and go out to eat dinner in a fancy restaurant. Nobody cared, no one bothered us, we were never asked to do anything. We felt like we were the only four people in the world, and it was absolutely wonderful.

There is something magical about being alone in a motorhome with just your husband and your two small children. This unexpected trip was a personal gift given to our young family by God; and we created memories that will live in our hearts for the rest of our lives.

This trip had not only helped Andrew move on, but it permanently united the four of us as a real family. Our church ministry functioned at such a fast pace; it was incredible to be able to just slow down and enjoy our lives for a few weeks. We all loved the campgrounds, the boys liked sleeping in their own bunk beds, taking walks, holding hands, and roasting marshmallows over a real campfire. We did not have a plan as to how far to go on our adventure; we just believed we would know when it was time to head home.

As we traveled through town after town, we noticed holiday decorations adorning every store. There were sparkling Christmas lights, nativity scenes with messages reminding everyone that Jesus was the Reason for the Season. Each town shared the excitement and joy of Christmastime. It was like driving through a holiday wonderland.

Once again taking a family road trip was the perfect answer to a very difficult situation. It is amazing how just getting away from the stress of everyday living can change your whole way of thinking. We all returned home completely different people than we were when we left.

We got back to Arlington a week before Christmas. Just in time to prepare our home for our very first Christmas together as a family. This Christmas was so magnificent, we could not have felt more blessed. My life had taken many unexpected twists and turns to get to this place, but I was finally spending my very first Christmas, as the wife of my knight-in-shining armor, Andrew Paul Brookshire the 3rd.

Thirteen

Meeting Billy Graham

On September 7, 1979, Andrew's ministry took on a whole new revelation. We had been married for a little over a year and although, Andrew had known since he was a young man that he had been called to be a pastor, that September changed his ministry forever.

In September 1979 we took the boys to Milwaukee, Wisconsin to participate in a large Billy Graham Crusade. Billy Graham was a powerful, American evangelist and an ordained Southern Baptist minister who became well-known internationally as a prominent evangelist Christian figure.

For many years Billy Graham was known as the most influential Christian leader of the 20th Century. His rallies attracted millions of people all over the globe. His popular appeal was the result of his extraordinary charisma, his forceful preaching, and his simple homespun message. His message was simple, "Anyone who repents of his sins and accepts Jesus Christ will be saved."

Billy Graham stated, "The Bible has 66 books written over a period of 1,600 years by 40 writers and yet the message is the same throughout." He always said, "The only way to heaven was through Christ." Billy Graham preached an unchanging message he firmly believed was meant for all humanity, "God has not changed, nor has the nature of the human heart changed."

At his large crusades, many ministers from several denominations came to help and train spiritual counselors. On September 7, 1979 Andrew and I went to a Five-day crusade to take part in one of the largest crusades that Billy Graham had ever had. Pastors came from everywhere to help with this 5-day event because Milwaukee was known as the beer capital of the world and it was usually a deathbed for evangelism.

The crusade drew 100,000 people to the Milwaukee County Stadium and the crusade had a profound and lasting impact on Christians in Southeastern Wisconsin. It transformed lives. You could see it in the large number of people whose lives were changed...people who would go on living a life of discipleship.

What impacted everyone most about Billy Graham was his integrity and his humility. Billy Graham was a humble and decent man. He was sincere and he was approachable. He had a profound impact on Andrew. Andrew was amazed to see the way people listened to Billy Graham and responded to him. Andrew's entire ministry took on new life after the crusade. Andrew saw it as a challenge to strengthen his ministry and his own personal effort to spread the gospel.

Andrew was always a very dynamic speaker, but after we returned from the crusade his ministry took on a new intensity. He was on fire for the Lord, he was on a mission, and you could hear it in every sermon he preached. He loved his church; he loved his people and he wanted to someday spend eternity with every one of them in heaven. Once again, the church continued to grow and more and more people from the area came to know the Lord. It was a fantastic time in our church ministry.

The Lord just continued to sanctify our lives; three days before our second anniversary, we were blessed with our treasured angel, Juliette Marie. Andrew was so excited to have a precious little girl named after his beloved mother, and Juliette was beautiful. She was a blessing from God because Andrew feared he would never be able to have children of his own, after the severe injuries he accrued in Vietnam.

The summer Juliette was born was considered the worst heat wave in the United States since 1954. The all-time highest temperatures were at the end of June. By July, Dallas-Fort Worth reported its highest temperatures of at least 100 degrees or higher for over 42 days. Memphis and Little Rock, Arkansas also recorded its longest streak of 100 plus degree days.

The heat wave was among the most destructive and most lethal natural disaster in U.S. history claiming at least 1,700 lives. For days everyone kept their children inside their houses, out of the hot sun. Luckily, our large old stone house stayed cool even on the hottest days, and of course the house was surrounded by tall trees. Arlington got hot, but it never reached the high temperature that some of the neighboring states did.

The boys loved having a new baby sister so they really did not mind staying inside the house for a few days. They held her, they kissed her continually, and she truly was beautiful, we could not help but just adore her. She was perfect.

The twins took turns rocking her to sleep at naptime. If she was on a blanket, on the floor one of the boys would lay beside her trying to make her smile by showing her colorful toys. Our baby girl never lacked for attention.

When Juliette was only five months old, I once again started having morning sickness and fourteen months after Juliette was born the Lord blessed us with our second precious angel; Margaret Elizabeth. Our family was finally complete.

Since the day we were married the twins had always been known as Sammy and Andy Brookshire, but we had never legally changed their names. We had left the twins with Samuel's last name, out of reverence to his family, but after both girls were born, we went to a lawyer and

Andrew legally adopted the boys so that all our children would have the same last name.

We changed their names to: Samuel Dean Peterson-Brookshire and Andrew Paul Peterson-Brookshire. Most people already called them Sammy Brookshire and Andy Brookshire, but we wanted everything to be legal.

Living in the parsonage behind the church was so convenient. Yet, at times we had visitors every hour of the day and night, because our home was so easy to access. I loved being a pastor's wife. I loved my family, and I loved my church. The Lord had blessed me ten times over, but with this large of a congregation Andrew was constantly busy doing weddings, funerals, baptisms, baby dedication and hospital visitations.

Although we tried to keep our life somewhat structured, we had unexpected interruptions all the time. When people are in an emergency situation, they want their pastor. Almost daily, people would call because they were in the hospital from a serious car accident, or sitting at the bedside of a loved one, or on their deathbed and did not want to die alone. They were scared, and the only person they wanted was Andrew; and Andrew took his ministry very seriously. Sometimes he would walk in the door for dinner and hurriedly eat, then he was out the door again because someone needed him.

Andrew was the ultimate prayer warrior for the Lord, that is why everyone wanted him with them when they were having problems. He sincerely believed in the power of prayer. He brought comfort to people just by praying with them. Our church witnessed miracle after miracle. We were truly living in an incredible time. Each day was a new beginning. Every morning we would wake up wondering what the Lord had in store for us for that day. As hectic as our lives were, I must admit we absolutely loved it.

When Andrew got a request, he went to be with his people. Andrew was probably the strongest Christian believer I had ever met in my life. Even after being married to him for several years, I still looked at him as if he were a saint. He loved serving the Lord, and he went to help his people whenever he was called; during the day or in the middle of the night. Oftentimes he would function on only 3 or 4 hours of sleep a night.

Once again, the church board was aware of the many life disruptions our family endured. We now had several ministers on full time at the church, and they decided it was time to take some of the pressure off Andrew, because he had carried the responsibility for way too long. Since Andrew became Head Pastor, the church had grown astonishingly; we even had several families that came in from the other side of Boston each week.

Everyone knew that a large part of the constant church growth was because of Andrew's personal involvement with each family, but he was getting tired and he needed to slow down and spend more time with his own family.

The board decided it was time to organize several of our associate pastors to answer many of Andrew's urgent emergency request. They also trained several new associates to be counselors and mediators in family affairs. Although, Andrew loved being in the middle of everything, we decided it was time to move out of the parsonage and get our own house.

When the twins were in fourth grade, we bought a beautiful house on the other side of town. Andrew had lived in the parsonage since he was twenty-five years old and we knew it was time to buy our own home for our growing family. Also, the church board felt it would help free up more of Andrew's family time if he didn't live in the back of the church property.

FOURTEEN

Life

We found a beautiful old three-story home only three blocks from the house where Keith and I had been raised. The old mansion had been restored and it needed very few upgrades. We loved our new home. Each of our kids had their own bedroom and we had a huge manicured fenced in yard with shrubs, trees, and lots of flowers. It was the perfect place to raise our family, and it was just the right distance from the church; close, but not next-door.

After we got settled in our new home Andrew and I decided it was time to start a new tradition. We planned a family reunion to take place every July during the Revere Beach International Sand Sculpturing Festival. The Revere Beach is the first American public beach in the United States.

Every year in the month of July they have a huge Sand Sculpturing Festival with over a million people attending.

It is a three-day event that is open to the public and it draws crowds from all over the world. Thousands of people walk the boardwalk to see the giant sand sculptures, the beach entertainment, and the fireworks and food.

Many of my family members stayed at our house, but we arranged for other families who came to stay at our hotel. The first year we had the reunion all the grandparents and many of the aunts, uncles and cousins came from both families. Even many of Samuel's family members came. The Revere Sand Sculpturing Festival was a big event for the Boston area, so it was a great time for a family reunion because there was a lot to see and do.

The Revere Beach is best known for the Lightning roller coaster and the Cyclone roller coaster. The Lightning roller coaster was built by Harry Davis and the all-steel roller coaster was the most terrifying of its time. The beach is about 5 miles north of downtown Boston. It is over three-miles long and is best known for its noisy arcades and famous fried foods.

We continued to have the reunion each year, for over twenty-five years, many relatives came ever year, some came ever few years. As the families grew, we often had new people, but at least everyone knew they were welcome. Many people planned their vacations around the July reunion in Arlington. Andrew absolutely loved having the family reunions because my family, and

Samuel's family were the only real relatives Andrew had. Since his mom's death, he only had his dad.

My children and I flew back to Idaho at least once a year to be with family so, although we were 2,700 miles apart, we got together often. Andrew usually came with us, and he stayed for a few days and then returned to be at the church.

The kids and I stayed in Idaho for several weeks at a time. That gave the twins time to visit with both sets of grandparents. Although, I must admit Samuel's parents treated Juliette and Margaret just as if they were their grandchildren too. We were a truly blessed family, and every one of the kids called both sets of grandparents Grandma and Grandpa. That is all they had ever known.

As the kids got older, we would often leave Sam and Andy in Idaho to stay an extra couple of weeks with each of the grandparents after we headed home. Although, the twins had never known their biological Father, I wanted them to always remember his family because they had been such a big part of their birth, and the first few years of their lives. To them Andrew had always been their only father, but Samuel was a very prominent, Christian doctor and I wanted them to know him through his family.

When the twins were in their Junior year of High School, we were blessed to inherit an extra son, Sam's best friend, Robert Nielson. Rob came to stay at our house while his parents were on a trip overseas. It was December and as we decorated our home for the holiday season, we just included Rob in any of the events our family might be planning.

Rob had been Sam's best friend since they were little, and his family had attended our church most of Rob's life. So, it was not unusual for Rob to stay at our house while his parents traveled out of the country, on business trips. It was only a few days before Christmas and Rob's parents promised him, they would be home by Christmas Eve, but on December 20th, as we watched the evening news; we discovered that there had been a deadly plane crash in Cali, Columbia where Rob's parent had been traveling.

Andrew immediately called the airlines and he discovered that earlier that day on December 20, 1995, at 9:41 p.m. Eastern Standard Time the Boeing 757-200, flying route N651AA crashed into a mountain near BUGA, Columbia. It was confirmed that the crash killed 151 of the 155 passengers and all 8 crew members. 4 passengers and a dog, in a dog carrier survived.

Rob's parents, Robert and Jenelle Neilson were listed on the passenger lists and they were not the names of the four survivors. Andrew was told that earlier that day the American Airlines Boeing 757-223 flight 965 had waited at the Miami Airport for transit passengers from the Northeast region. The plane finally arrived, but it was two hours behind schedule. The controller advised the flight crew to take the shortest approach route to recover the two-hour delay.

While changing the route, a crew member put 'R' into the computer. The computer changed the course and when the captain discovered the error, he told the co-pilot to turn right, but the plane had already strayed into the mountainous terrain.

Although the crew increased the engine power, the plane crashed while grazing the mountaintop without rising. Radio communication was lost after the crew last requested the Cali Airport for landing approach.

An eyewitness residing in the mountainous terrain, described the accident as he stated, "The airplane hit the west slope of the mountain at about 8,900 feet near Cali, and crashed and burst into flames." It was later described as the deadliest accident with a Boeing 757 at that time.

After we received the true conformation that Rob's parents had died in the plane crash, I sat with Rob for several hours and just held him in my arms, and listened to him sob. Although, he was much bigger than I was, I put my arms around his shoulders and rocked him back and forth, just like my mother did with me after Andrew left for Vietnam, and after we received word Andrew had been killed, and after we got word, that Samuel had died. I remember how comforting it was for me when my mother held me. It was a time when I felt all alone and lost and did not know how I could carry on, just like Rob was feeling now.

Andrew did the funeral for both of Rob's parents, and of course, Rob continued to live at our house for the next two years until he left for college. Andrew and I always had room for one more, it was just the way we lived. We often made a place for teens to stay at our house for a few days when they had nowhere else to go.

Rob's situation was different, he had permanently lost everyone. So, from that day forward, I told everyone I had three boys and two girls, because we were now Rob's only family, and nothing could ever change that. We were the only parents he would have for the rest of his life.

Robert and Jenelle had left Rob a large insurance policy, and the airlines also distributed thousands of dollars to the families who had lost loved ones in the crash. So, he had plenty of money in the bank to pay for his college and help him with his future. He also had their nice home to live in when he returned from college, and was ready to be out on his own.

When you have children, you often gage time by the age that the children were at a certain time that something happened. I do not know how people who never have children ever remember certain life events. For instance, I remember losing my grandparents from Texas, in a car accident when the twins were in the sixth grade. Juliette was in second grade when Keith and Margie had their fourth baby, and Margaret was in first grade when our family flew to Hawaii, and of course, Rob was a junior in High School when his parents died, and he came to live with us. Rob had lived with us for about six months when

Andrew took the entire family to Disney World for a comforting vacation.

While raising children, your life is chaotically changing every day; one son needs new football cleats, one needs different basketball shorts, one of the girls outgrew her ballet slippers while your youngest daughter needs to be at a swim meet at the same time Samuel is playing basketball at the school. We were very proud of our children and everything that they accomplished. We loved going to ballet recitals, swim meets and basketball and football games. Rob was into soccer so we went to his games too.

Our life was just go, go, go... but I wouldn't have changed one day of our wonderful tumultuous family life. Between the church and all the sports activities, it takes a super mom and a super dad to get everything accomplished, but we had volunteered for the challenge and somehow, we always got everything done. Raising our family was the most rewarding purpose of our lives, and we would not have traded that time for anything in this world.

The sad part of being a busy parent is that with each passing day your precious children are learning to be independent of you, so that they can one day grow up and be out on their own. One by one they take drivers training and get a car. They graduate from high school and go on to college. They no longer need someone to drive them everywhere, and they no longer need your help with homework, or advice on anything they are doing.

Within a few short years they are all grown and out on their own. Sometimes I think parents should have ten children so that there is someone at home for many years, and they do not all grow up and move out at once.

As each child moved out of the house, a small piece of me disappeared along with them, until the busy ambitious person that I had been all my life was no longer necessary. That was a very difficult time for me, I did not know how to be just a wife, because I had learned to be a busy wife and a mother most of my adult life.

In a marriage, you learn to make sacrifices when you are raising your family, and once your family is grown you must learn to rebuild your marriage over and over again. Older couples need to learn to listen to each other and apologize when they need to. They must learn to make time for each other, because each other is all that they have.

With all the kids grown, we then had our giant three-story, six-bedroom house with just Andrew and me and our old cat, Pickles. I had never looked forward to being empty nesters, and the day that Margaret got married was one of the saddest days of my life. I will be honest, my heart was broken, I was happy for her, I loved our new son-in-law, Tom, but I felt very lost and lonely and I knew my busy-life would never be the same again.

Samuel had followed in his paternal father's footsteps. Like his father, his grandfather, and his great-grandfather he went to medical school and became a doctor in Boise, Idaho. Juliette and her husband took over the management of the Arlington Suites Hotel, and Margaret and her husband Tom were both school teachers. Andy got married and became a Boston High School football coach, and a youth leader at a small church out of Boston, and Rob graduated from college and became a lawyer, and married a girl from the area.

Margaret had only been married a few months when 19 terrorists, hijacked four commercial airplanes and flew two of them into the World Trade Center, one into the Pentagon, and crashed the fourth one in an empty field.

The first plane, flight 11 took off at 7:59 from Logan International airport in Boston, Massachusetts with 76 passengers aboard, 11 crew members and 5 hijackers. The hijackers knew the planes would be full of fuel because they were headed to Los Angeles. They flew flight 11 into the World Trade Center.

At 8:15 United Airlines Flight 175 left Boston and headed for California. There were 51 passengers aboard, with 9 crew members, and 5 hijackers. Flight 175 was the second plane to hit the World Trade Center.

At 8:20 A. M. American Airlines Flight 77 took off from Dulles airport out of Washington D. C. It was also headed for Los Angeles. It had 53 passengers on board, with 6 crew members and 5 hijackers, and it hit the Pentagon.

The third airplane, United Airlines flight 93 crashed in a field in Pennsylvania.

The terrorist attack disturbed all of us. Everyone was in shock, but one name in particular caught Andrew's attention when he saw it on television. The man was Max Beilke who had been killed by the terrorist, when they flew the Boeing 757 into the Pentagon during the attacks. Andrew recognized the name because Max Beilke was the very last soldier to leave Vietnam when the war had ended. His departure was caught on live television as he boarded a C-130 transport to come home.

After fighting and surviving wars in Korea and in Vietnam, he was killed 28 years later by a terrorist flying a plane into the Pentagon. Beilke was a deputy of the Retirement Services Division for the military, and he was just visiting the Pentagon that day when the giant 757 flew into the building killing 184 people plus 5 hijackers.

U.S. Airspace was immediately shut down under operation yellow ribbon. All civilian aircraft were ordered to land at the nearest airport. Our country was once again in overwhelming sorrow and turmoil, all planes were grounded, and people were afraid to go out of their homes.

There were so many things we did not understand; like why did this happen, will another disaster occur, does this mean we are at war in our own country? Many people in our church had friends or family members that were killed in the World Trade center or were traveling on one of the planes.

Ellen Johnson's brother was one of the firemen that died, and the Smith family lost two of their children that worked in the World Trade Center, and the Reynold's family lost a sister and her husband that were flight attendants on flight 11. Matt Phillips, a young newly married member of our church was on his way to the airport to catch a flight to California for a big business trip when he had a flat tire, and missed his flight. He would have been on flight 175, the second plane to hit the World Trade Center.

The entire country lived in fear, because we felt so vulnerable, and we did not know how to defend ourselves. The people of Arlington were terrified because two of the planes that hit the World Trade Center had come from the airport in Boston, only seven miles away.

Within a few days people all over America started putting flags on their cars, trucks, work vehicles, in front of their businesses, churches and on every house. We were showing the world that Americans were standing united together.

By October 7, 2001, a U.S. led coalition began attacks on the Taliban that controlled Afghanistan. President George W. Bush launched a 'Global War on Terror.' It was dubbed 'Operation Enduring Freedom' in U. S. military parlance, the invasion in Afghanistan was intended to target the terrorists mastermind Osama bin Laden, the leader responsible for the destruction of the twin Towers.

My first thought, was to hold my children close, and protect them, and never let them out of my sight. Yet, that was not possible, because they were no longer mine to protect. They were all in their own homes taking care of their own families, and they did not need my help.

I once heard a speaker at a conference say, "You can tell when you did a good job raising your children, when they become good Christian adults, and get out on their own and no longer require your help." For some reason that statement did not really comfort me, because I loved raising my family and having everyone close, I never minded being exhausted each evening from taking care of everyone that I love.

With all the kids married we eventually had twelve grandchildren, including Rob's two children, but I never grew accustomed to living in our giant quiet house without all of them around. Although Andrew had always been the love of my life, my heart often felt empty and lost, and I wasn't sure who I was supposed to be now that I was growing older.

My grandchildren came over often, and I became more active in the church, I spoke at several meetings, and I learned to make quilts, but I sometimes felt like I was just finding things to do to keep busy. Andrew and I flew back to Idaho at least three times a year to see Sam, my parents and Keith and Margie, but I do not think I ever truly got over having that huge house and not having my family at home.

Fifteen

A trip of A lifetime

Andrew's dad had been sick for several months when he had a massive stroke and passed away in the middle of the night. This was a terrible shock to Andrew, because he had always been so close to his dad, and his dad was the only blood relative that he had. His dad went to church with us every Sunday, and he had been coming over for dinner after church every Sunday since we got married. As disturbing as his dad's death was to both of us, Andrew told the church board that he wanted to personally do his father's funeral.

Andrew was a very disciplined speaker; and of course, he had done several very difficult funerals throughout his ministry. He told the church board, that no one knew the wonderful things about his father like he did, so he wanted to do the service himself. My heart was broken because his dad had been like a second father to me, but Andrew did a commendable job honoring his father at his funeral.

He and his dad had been through so much together throughout their lives, and for several weeks after his dad's death Andrew seemed very distant, he had a lot on his mind and he would sit for hours and just quietly think and pray.

One of things that I admired about my husband was that through all the years that he had been the main minister at our church, he never felt like he was the head of the church; he knew God was. I think that is why the people wanted him to remain for so many years, because everyone recognized his true heart. My husband had been the Lead Pastor since he was 25 years old, and it is unheard of for a pastor to remain at one church for his entire ministry, but he was very devoted to his people and he never chose to go anywhere else.

Yet, throughout the past ten years or so he had handed many of his duties over to other ministers in the church. We were both getting older, and the death of Andrew's father had really made an impact on both of us. Andrew felt he had several decisions he needed to make. Andrew knew how much his father had missed his mother, Juliette, when she passed away at such a young age. His father had so many regrets about the things they never got to do together.

A few weeks after his father's funeral, Andrew came home and told me, "We are at an age that we need to take more time to enjoy our life, and start doing more things together, just the two of us." We started going out on dates again; we would drive into Boston for a romantic private dinner or take walks in the park or stop at local ice cream shop for a hot fudge sundae.

He even bought me a brand-new little sports car for my birthday. He got me a shiny little red Mazda MX 5 Miata. It was probably the cutest car I had ever seen in my life. It was a total surprise, because it was completely different than the big old Dodge Caravan that I used to drive and haul the family around in.

We had never really had much time since we got married to be alone and just do things together, with just the two of us. When we got married, I already had the twins. So, now with the family grown, and we were all alone, it was our time to live; to hold hands and walk along the boardwalks and just be us. Andrew had always been so romantic, but this was a special time in our lives, it was as if we were eighteen again.

For years the church had been our life, but we talked it over and prayed about it, and Andrew finally decided it was time for him to step down, and fully retire. He had numerous pastors following close behind, and of course, Andrew had not preached every service for several years, but he performed most of the weddings, funerals, and baby dedications. The church had two morning services, plus Saturday, Sunday, and Wednesday evening. Our church was well-known in the community, and it had something going on at all hours of the day and most evenings.

We had several men's and ladies' Bible studies, a large choir, several youth groups, college age groups, singles, a preschool, and we even developed a private Christian school for ages Kindergarten through 8th grade.

Also, countless larger classrooms were utilized during the week nights for different self-help classes. The church doors were open all the time. Andrew had organized many of the groups, but over the past few years he had gradually stepped back once he got them started.

The church gave him a huge retirement party. People came from miles away just to let Andrew know how much he had helped them, and how he had changed their lives. Hundreds of people had been saved because of Andrew's dedication. It was wonderful to see all the old faces from the past, but it was also a sad time of goodbyes to dear friends that had been such a huge part of our lives since we were teenagers in the church youth group.

Many of the older people that came to the retirement party, were members that we had not seen at the church in years. One man was 102 years old. Some came in wheelchairs, some with walkers, some had to be brought to the church by their adult children. They said they wanted to see Andrew and me again, to say goodbye. They had been there many years ago when we had our wedding, so of course they could not miss 'our' retirement party. Ever since we got married, I have remained totally involved in the church. When a minister retires after being at one church for many years it truly is a retirement for both the minister and his wife. Many people from our original congregation are now all alone because they have lost their spouses, and of course Andrew had done most of their family's funeral services. They came to say thank you one last time.

A week after he retired, instead of being sad and depressed Andrew went to the travel agency and collected stacks of travel brochures. He brought home pamphlets of exotic places all over the world. He was so excited he told me he would take me anywhere I wanted to go. I had never seen him so giddy; he was ready to take off and travel around the world and visit every country.

After studying the colorful brochures, we decided to start with Italy, because I had always dreamed of going to Italy. The more we planned the more excited we both became. This would be an adventure of a lifetime. We were no longer confined to getting home to the church, because Andrew was truly retired and we had no children at home that needed us, so we could be gone for as long as we wanted to be.

Being the Lead Pastor of a large church can be very demanding and Andrew always felt he should quickly return home to Arlington, because he might be needed. He now realized his job was done, and he could pass the position on to one of the younger ministers. He felt his commitment was completed.

Although, we had been blessed to be able to travel throughout America; we were ready to take our time and see the world and travel to other countries. We would start with Italy, then go onto Germany, France, and Spain, that would be the first countries on our agenda.

For the second part of our trip, we planned to travel to India, China, and then on to Vietnam. Ever since Andrew was in the Vietnam War, he had wanted to return to see the country at a better time.

After we decided to go to Vietnam, I went to visit two of my young Vietnamese friends, Jenny, and Anna. They were both born in Vietnam and I wanted to get some information about their country. Since Andrew had gone to war there, I was a little apprehensive of him going back again. Although Jenny and Anna loved living in America, they returned to their homeland every few years to visit family members who are still living there. Jenny's parents are both living and working in America, and although, Jenny's parents have been here for many years, her mother has never learned to speak English.

Anna's mother had remained in Vietnam for many years. Anna told me that her mother would soon be coming to the United States to marry her old sweetheart, a Vietnamese neighbor boy who had moved to America with his family after the war. Anna said that her mother had not seen her old neighbor for many years, but they had recently got in contact with each other again. She said they had been childhood sweethearts and had planned to get married, but the man's parents brought him all the way to America, so they both ended up marrying other people at that time. Now that they are older and alone, they plan to get married and live in the United States.

Jenny and Anna were really excited for me to go and see their wonderful country. They were born after the war, but they had heard stories and had seen old pictures. They said their beautiful country is nothing like it was when the Vietnam War was going on. They are both proud of their birthplace, and they were anxious for me to go and visit there.

They told me how totally different the Vietnamese culture is from the American culture. They said in Vietnam the man is the head of the house, and he is always right. You are not allowed to disagree with him. Also, the children are expected to send money home to support their aging parents.

The Vietnamese parents support the children while they are young, and then the children are expected to support the parents when they grow old. It was interesting hearing about their beloved country. I felt much better about us going to Vietnam after talking with my two young friends.

When Andrew was in Vietnam, he was on a special mission as a 'Tunnel Rat.' He recently discovered that the tunnels that he crawled through during the war were now part of the Vietnam War Memorial Park in Ho Chi Minh City (formerly Saigon). It was now a popular tourist attraction where visitors could crawl through sections of the tunnels that had once been used by the 'Tunnel Rats,' like Andrew. Now there are no mines, booby traps, large rats, or poisonous snakes. It opened to the public on Veterans Day 1996. During the war they could burrow 50 feet underground and sometimes contain up to four different levels.

The 'Tunnel Rats' had specialized training, so there were never more than 100 'Tunnel Rats' in the Vietnam War at any one time. There were around 700 total that had been trained as 'Tunnel Rats' during the war, but being a 'Tunnel Rat' was a very dangerous job, so several were killed and wounded. Most tunnels were 6 feet deep and 100 feet long.

Andrew had lost a lot of friends in the war, so I was kind of surprised when he wanted to go back and visit. He said he wanted to return during peace time so that he could see it in different circumstances. 997 soldiers were killed on their first day in Vietnam. 1,448 soldiers were killed on the last day in Vietnam. There are 31 sets of brothers that were killed in the Vietnam War and they have their names on the Vietnam Wall in Washington D.C.

A lot of the soldiers that returned home after Vietnam were rejected and ridiculed by their friends and neighbors. They ended up leaving their families, and many became alcoholics and drug addicts, and they had a hard time adjusting to civilian life again. People did not honor the returning Vietnam soldiers like they did other soldiers in other wars.

Andrew had been severely wounded there, but the Lord had blessed him so richly after he recovered that his position was entirely different when he returned home. He had been through such a strange situation; he had been pronounced dead, buried, and then found alive, so everyone was delighted when he came back. Also, he had been in the hospital recuperating for several months after he returned to America, and he was so thankful to be alive that his entire attitude was different than many of the other returning soldiers. After he was released from the hospital, he went directly into preparing for the ministry, so he adjusted to civilian life much easier than so many of the others did.

After leaving Beijing, China we headed for Vietnam. When we arrived at the front area of the tunnels there is a large welcome sign to the Chu Chi tunnels. There are several exhibits around the site, and a souvenir shop and a firing range where people can shoot guns. It truly was different than he remembered.

Andrew told me, "The duty of the 'Tunnel Rat' was to slide along into the tunnels entrance and search for the enemy and any other valuable intelligence." He said, "The 'Tunnel Rats' were Americans, Australians, New Zealanders and South Vietnamese soldiers who performed underground search and destroy missions." He shook his head, "It was a very dangerous mission. We often went by smell, touch, and hearing; and the giant rats that lived inside the tunnels were terrifying. Many of them were the size of dogs." He covered his face before going on, "The big rats that lived inside the tunnels would often climb all over us in the dark, and we had to remain totally silent. We could not make a sound or the enemy would know we were there. At least, 25 to 50 American soldiers died each year of snake bites."

He continued, "Most of the 'Tunnel Rat' soldiers were thin like I was, some were smaller, but we also needed to be intelligent and skilled at hand-to-hand combat. Our job was to kill, capture or extort the Viet Cong with explosives." He smiled as he said, "We were often referred to as combat engineers. We were trained at an Australian Army School of military Engineering, located 20 miles west of Sydney, Australia."

He slowly shook his head back and forth then went on, "We were unable to communicate with our families while we there in training. Everything was classified. That is where I was when the false information of my death was sent back to my family in America. By the time I was once again able to write home, my family had buried a soldier they thought was me, my mother had passed away, and my dad had gone to our family cabin for several months to try to cope with our deaths."

He went on, "1968 was one of the bloodiest years for American troops in the war. It was estimated that over 181,000 Viet Cong and North Vietnamese were killed. 27,915 South Vietnamese and 14,584 Americans and 979 Australians, New Zealanders, South Koreans, and Thais."

As we sat there at the front of the entrance in the area where Andrew had been critically wounded, he stared off into space. Then he recalled, "I had just come out of the tunnel and rejoined my unit when we were attacked by the enemy right in this area. All I remember is the bright explosion of the white phosphorus bomb, and everything around us burst in to hot flames including all the soldiers in front of me. I knew I was severely wounded, and several of my buddies had fallen back on top of me, and at first, they were all groaning and screaming and then it was total silence, and I knew they were dead."

He started getting very emotional as he continued telling me, "Kathryn, I lay there under a mass of dead soldiers trying not to move or make any noise. I kept repeating our memory verse inside my head: 1 Thessalonians 5:16-18, Rejoice always, pray continually, give thanks in all circumstances; for this is God's will for you in Christ Jesus. I repeated it over and over and over without making a sound. I remained perfectly still, hoping that someone from our unit would come to bury the bodies and find me.

But the first soldiers to come along were enemy soldiers, I was absolutely terrified, but I pretended to be dead so they left me alone. All they could see were burned dead bodies, I was buried underneath them, but I was silent so they assumed I was dead too."

My beloved husband covered his face with both hands and then looked up toward the sky and said, "As I lay there bleeding and critically wounded, I diligently prayed and talked to God." He continued, "I had just turned nineteen years old, I was all alone, covered in dead bodies, in the middle of the pitch-black jungle and I was scared to death. Praying to the Lord was my only comfort."

Andrew stopped for a second to compose himself before going on, “I pleaded with God that if he got me back home, I would spend my life serving him.” Andrew looked around at the area and smiled at me and said, “I instantly felt a calmness come over me, and I was no longer afraid, because I knew God was right here with me. He saved me, and that is the last thing I remember. Somehow, I was found and I was sent back to the states, and I served my Lord and devoted my life to the church, and to you and our family.”

With tears in his eyes, my sweet husband then looked at me and said, “Kathryn, I should have died that day, I do not even know how I got back to America. All I remember is waking up in a hospital in San Francisco, and I don’t even know how I got there.”

Then Andrew once again closed his eyes and prayed out loud, “Oh Lord, please forgive us for the many evils that go on during wartime. Evils that as a soldier we are often forced to take part in. Forgive us for the deaths and destruction that took place in this land, and Lord, I can never praise you enough for sparing my life, and for granting me more time to fulfil my life’s purpose.”

As eerie as it was for me to be sitting in the exact area where Andrew had once laid with dead bodies protecting him from his enemies; I could tell it was helping him to heal from his unbearable memories. The more he talked and prayed the calmer he became. I then realized why he wanted to return to Vietnam; to this place. He wanted to come back to where his life was personally touched by God and resurrected. As I looked around at the beautiful landscape, it was unreal to think that this area was once a deadly war zone where 58,000 men and women were killed or left missing. My friends Jenny and Anna were right, Vietnam is a completely different country than it was when Andrew was fighting the war.

Andrew kept reminiscing, "One of the oddest things I remember about coming to Vietnam when I was eighteen, was we left San Francisco and flew to Vietnam. The flight took 22 hours and because of the time change we arrived in Vietnam the same day we left."

When Andrew was ready to crawl through the tunnels, we went with several other people, and we met with a guide who instructed everyone the specific way to enter the hole. The guide entered the hole feet first and then he held the lid high above his head, and then he bent at the knee so the rest of his body could slide through. The guide told everyone that many of the tunnels have been enlarged so that tourist could get through easier. Even being made larger the caves were very claustrophobic. I could hardly wait to duck-walk through the walkways, and climb up the metal ladder to get back above ground.

It was so bizarre to visualize that Andrew and the other 'Tunnel Rats' had once crept through these same tunnels. The tunnels were now well-lit and considerably cleaner than they were in Andrew's day as a soldier. Yet as odd as it was climbing through the tunnels, I was glad that he chose to share this 'lost' part of his life with me.

After we left the tunnels, we stopped at the gift shop and purchased several Vietnam memorial gold coins that were each beautifully displayed in small wooden boxes. We purchased one for every one of our children and for each of our grandchildren.

We then went into town and visited the Factory Contemporary Art Center. It was one of the places my friends Jenny and Ann had told me about. It specialized in contemporary art, Vietnam Visual Art that dates back as far as the stone ages and includes handcrafts, woodwork, clay, and bronze as well as paintings and sculptures.

The next day we visited the War Remnants Museum. It contains exhibits relating to the First Indonesian War and the Vietnam War. We also, went to the Ben Thanh Market located in the center of Ho Chi Minh City, Vietnam in District 1. The market is one of the earliest surviving structures in Saigon and it is an important symbol of the city. The Ben Thanh Market is a famous destination for many local and foreign tourists from all around the world. The market welcomes more than 10,000 visitors each day to shop and visit. The market has 1,500 booths with more than 6,000 small businesses.

It was amazing to visit the modern Vietnam of today. It was hard to imagine this beautiful place as a battle field, but for the surviving soldiers of the Vietnam War, they will never forget the horrors of that time. Vietnam is now ranked as one of the safest countries in the world for travelers.

Our entire trip was fantastic. It is interesting to see how other people in this world live. We visited exotic places as well as people that lived in huts. When we were in the Vietnam jungle, I thought of Samuel, the twin's dad, because I imagined the area in Africa where he had gone with 'The Doctors Without Borders' was much like the forest in Vietnam.

It made me sad to think how Samuel suffered and died from Malaria in a remote jungle just like Vietnam, thousands of miles away from home and his family. Yet, he died doing what he chose to do. It is odd, but my life had been so perfect with Andrew that I rarely thought of Samuel. Maybe, it was because I had always remained so close with all of Sam's relatives, it was as if he was never really gone. He lived on in the twins and in his family.

On our trip we ate in elegant restaurants, traveled with the wealthiest people of the world, but we also walked on dirt roads and sat with people who had never been out of their remote villages. I loved seeing the different cultures, landscapes, and nationalities of this earth.

It truly made me appreciate the wonderful years the Lord had granted Andrew and me. Sometimes you need to travel the globe to be grateful for the safe, comfortable life you have been given.

As I sat next to my Andrew on the plane on our way back to the states, my heart filled with joy. Even after all these years, he was still my forever love, and I am so grateful for our life story. In a marriage you must take the bad with the good and learn from the bad and be thankful for the good times.

Marriage requires many compromises; you must overlook each other's faults. You forgive mistakes and endure many problems. You spend years learning to understand one another, and raising a family can be exhausting. Love is not a matter of luck. It is mutual giving, compromise, shared dreams, care, respect, mercy, and patience. I still looked at Andrew through starry eyes. I silently smiled because to me he was flawless. His hair was slowly turning gray, and his distinguished laugh lines now appear as wrinkles, but I still think he is the kindest, gentlest, decent, and most handsome man on this earth, and I thank God for him every day.

As I watched my husband sleep in the seat next to me, on the plane ride home, I reminisced about the wondrous things we had seen in the past several weeks: I thought of Rome, Italy with the Vatican, and the ancient ruins. I thought of Brandenburg, Germany, and the many war sites from WWII. I thought of Paris, France, and the art museums including the Louvre and Eiffel Tower. We visited Madrid, Spain, the home of the Royal Palace. In India we saw the Taj Mahal and the Holy City of Varanasi. In China the Great Wall of China, The Forbidden City and The Imperial Palace in Beijing, and of course the tunnels of Vietnam.

As I watched my treasured husband sleep, I thought back to the day I received the letter from Andrew's father telling me that Andrew had been killed in Vietnam and that I was to move on with my life. My heart was destroyed, then I married Samuel and within a short time I received word that he was gone too.

I remember sitting all by myself in my house in Idaho, pregnant and alone wondering what I was going to do. It was probably the darkest time of my life. Now as I sit on a giant plane, next to the love of my life, heading back to Arlington to my beautiful home after touring much of the world, I am overwhelmingly thankful. After I received word that Samuel died, I could have never guessed what great plans the Lord was preparing for my life. My children, my husband, my church, my grandchildren, my friends...I have been truly blessed.

Sixteen

The Joy of the Lord

We had only been back in the states for a short while when one afternoon after shopping with my daughters, I came home to find Andrew asleep in his chair sitting at his desk. That was so out of character for him. He never fell asleep during the day. When I woke him up, he said he had been experiencing shortness of breath and chills. It wasn't until then that I noticed that he had lost weight since we got back, and I realized he complained of being tired all the time. I had been so busy getting everything back in order after our world travels that I had not really noticed that he had been acting different since we got home.

When I asked him about it, he sluffed it off as exhaustion from our trip, he was never one to complain, and he promised he would check with the doctor in a few weeks. Several days passed and he appeared to be getting worse each day. He just seemed exhausted all the time, and he was so tired he kept forgetting things he was doing.

At first, we laughed about it, but it was becoming frightening to me. For instance, he would slowly walk into the kitchen to get a glass of water, then just stand at the sink, and stare out the window for several minutes. Soon he would turn around, shake his head back and forth then walk into the den. I began noticing him doing things like this all day long.

Then he started itching all over. He was scratching himself so badly, he started having painful burning everywhere he itched. He kept having unexpected fevers and every night he had horrible night sweats and he would wake up wringing wet.

He was really starting to scare me, and I got so I was afraid to let him out of my sight. He no longer felt like driving, he was just too exhausted. If we went anywhere, he would have me drive, but we usually just stayed home so he could rest.

I finally made him an appointment with the doctor. They told me to bring him in on the following Monday. He seemed so frail that at times he had a hard time getting up from his chair. I silently cried when I was alone. I knew something terrible was going on. This was my Andrew, my hero, my manly, brave, strong, courageous warrior, and he was failing right before my eyes. It was happening so quickly, and I was powerless to do anything to help him.

Early Monday morning our son Andy came over to help me get Andrew to the doctor. I had already notified each of our children that their father had not been feeling well, and Andy and I were taking him into the doctor to have him checked out.

After the doctor examined Andrew, he sent him by ambulance to Massachusetts General Hospital in Boston to run a bunch of tests. Five days later after the tests were complete, two doctors met with Andy, Juliette, Margaret, Rob, and I to let us know what they had found.

We were told that Andrew had gotten continually worse each day since he had entered the hospital. We were told that he slept most of the time and he had not been talking at all. We had not been allowed in his room, but we were told that his condition was very serious.

The doctors said they had concluded the tests and they told us that my sweet Andrew had all the effects of Agent Orange. The tests showed that somehow it had been contained inside his body, in a tumor for over forty years, and it was beginning to create a number of life-threatening conditions including cardiac problems, seizures and acute renal failure.

One of the doctors, Dr. Swenson was a specialist with the military on the effects of Agent Orange, that is why he had been called in to talk with us. He said, "The harmful ingredient in Agent Orange is Dioxin. Dioxin can remain in adipose tissue for decades after exposure. Dioxin could have a direct toxic effect on the brain, or it could act indirectly by impairing blood circulation or increasing the risk of other diseases that in time increase dementia."

Dr. Swenson told us, "Agent Orange has been found to persist after 50 years in water or soil of southern Vietnam. Dioxin from Agent Orange, sprayed by the U.S. military during the Vietnam War is still poisoning people today. Roughly, 300 thousand Vietnam veterans have died from Agent Orange exposure; that is almost 5 times as many as the 58 thousand who died in combat."

He continued, "Agent Orange, is an herbicide and defoliant chemical, and it was one of the 'tactical use' Rainbow Herbicides. It was used by the military as part of its herbicide warfare program, 'Operation Ranch Hand' during the Vietnam War from 1962 to 1971. Scientists have found that tumors in the prostate may remain dormant for decades. The growth is really slow, like Andrews. As the cancerous tumor enlarges and invades surrounding tissues it may grow into a blood vessel, causing bleeding and that can only be found by testing."

The doctor was very blunt, "Agent Orange is the most infamous of the 'rainbow herbicide' and its lingering toxicity continues to affect those exposed. It was designed to defoliate areas used by the enemy as cover for ambushes, as well as to destroy enemy subsistence crops. The U. S. sprayed these herbicides in Vietnam, usually from helicopters or low-flying aircraft, but sometimes from backpacks, boats, or trucks.

The jungle in Vietnam was so thick the enemy had a tactical advantage. To counter this advantage the Americans launched operation 'Ranch Hand' employing chemical herbicides and defoliants in enormous quantities to deprive the enemy of places to hide. U.S. aircraft were deployed to douse roads, rivers, canals, rice paddies and farmland with powerful mixtures of herbicides. During the process crops and water sources used by the non-combatant native population of South Vietnam were also hit."

He went on, "In all 20 million gallons of herbicides were used, its active ingredients caused plants to 'defoliate' or lose their leaves. Agent Orange contained Dioxin that had immediate and long-term effects. Dioxin accumulates in fatty tissue in the bodies of fish, birds, and other animals. Most human exposure is through foods such as meats, poultry, dairy products, eggs, shellfish, and fish. Studies done on laboratory animals have proven that Dioxin is highly toxic even in minute doses. It is universally known to be a carcinogen (a cancer-causing agent). Dioxin is linked to type 2-diebetes, immune system disruption, nerve disorders, muscular dysfunction, hormone disruption and heart disease."

The doctor wanted us to know, "A class-action lawsuit was filed on behalf of 2.4 million veterans who were exposed to Agent Orange during their service in Vietnam. Agent Orange accounted for more than half of the total volume of herbicides deployed. One of the key ingredients, Dioxin, is highly toxic even in tiny quantities. Operation 'Ranch

Hand' deployed about 375 pounds of Dioxin over an area about the size of Massachusetts. Thus, containing the entire ecosystem and exposing millions of people on both sides of the war to horrifying long-term effects, including skin diseases and cancers among those exposed. The chemical defoliants used during the Vietnam War are complex internationally debated, and continues to the present day."

Dr. Swenson then moved in closer to the group, and sadly stated, "I am sorry to inform you but I think it is time for you to call all your family members to let them know that Andrew has all the signs and symptoms that suggest he is in his final days of life. He has weakness, exhaustion, and a need to continually sleep. His charts show that he has had significant weight loss in the past few months, with no signs of infection or reason for his weight loss. The tests show he has muscle thinning, and we can tell by his evaluation that he has terminal hemorrhaging, and that is usually caused by the spreading of the tumor into the blood vessel."

The doctor continued, "Andrew is no longer responding to our questions. One of the things that we have discovered at this stage, is that most patients can hear, but they can no longer speak. Breathing is difficult for him and he has developed a drop in body temperature and blood pressure."

Later that evening Sam and his wife, Kari flew in from Idaho to say goodbye to his beloved father. I was absolutely in shock, because within just a few short months my life had gone from date nights with my precious Andrew, a new sports car, and a vacation of a lifetime around the world, to preparing a funeral for my loving husband. I could not think, I could not hear, I could barely breathe.

One by one each of our children went in alone to say goodbye to their father. When it was my time to go in, Andy and Sam walked beside me holding me up by each arm. They sat me down in a chair in front of Andrew, and then left the room so I could be alone with my esteemed husband one last time.

I sat in front of the bed for a few seconds and just watched him, but he never moved. Finally, I stood up to hold his hand for one last time, and I told him how much I loved him and I would meet him in heaven.

I started to cry and I told him, "Goodbye my love, I love you so much and I will miss you forever."

For the first time in a week, Andrew slowly opened his eyes and quietly whispered, "Kathryn Elizabeth Brookshire...You are my forever love." Then he closed his eyes and went to be with Jesus.

I screamed hysterically and the room went black as I fell backwards into my son, Sam's arms. Nothing seemed real, my world was spinning out of control, this could not be happening, but I knew it was, and I could not stop it.

Somehow over the next few weeks, the children and I made all the arrangements for their father's funeral, and

Andrew was buried in the Arlington National Cemetery, the United States military cemetery across the Potamic River from Washington D.C.

The church had a memorial bench made for him to be placed under the large oak tree, by the sidewalk next to the church. Andrew had served at the church for so many years, and he was loved by everyone in Arlington and many from the Boston Area, but he would always be 'My Andrew' to me.

For several days after the funeral, at least one of my children stayed with me so I would not have to be alone. After a few weeks, I started sorting through all of Andrew's military records. The family had gotten his records out for his funeral, but I had not looked through them. Before I started reading his information, I went to the back of my closet and found the precious teddy bear that Andrew had given me the night before he left for Vietnam, over forty years ago, when we were only eighteen years old. I had carefully preserved it in a large zipped plastic bag.

The bag also contained the two-piece heart necklaces. Both Andrew's half and my half were placed inside a small jewelry box in the bag. Down in one corner of the giant bag was the cardboard cut-out picture frame of Jesus that I had made at church camp the year that I met Andrew. I also had the letter he gave me that night, it was carefully placed up near the cuddly brown teddy bear with the huge red embroidered heart that said...My Forever Love. I held the teddy bear tight and wept into its fur, just like I had done so many times before. That bear had brought me comfort all throughout my lifetime.

After I collected my thoughts, I started going through his papers again. The first papers I came across were the records of the time when he was wounded and sent to the hospital in San Francisco. I had never seen any of this information before, this was the first time I had ever looked through his military records. Many of the documents were hard to understand, then I came across one paper that took my breath away, and I sat and stared at it for several seconds...I could not believe what I was seeing. The records showed the exact date that Andrew had been wounded in action; that horrible day when he was barely nineteen years old, and he had survived by playing dead laying silently under his deceased fellow soldiers.

Chills ran up my spine as I remembered what Andrew had told me when we had visited the tunnels on our trip to Vietnam a few months earlier. He told me that during the war when he had been critically wounded and was laying there dying, he made a promise to God. He promised God that he would be his faithful servant if God would spare his life, and let him get home to America. Andrew told me he knew he should have died there in the jungle along with all the other soldiers in his unit. He had no idea how he got back to the states, but he did get home, and for the rest of his life he kept the promise he had made to the Lord that day.

As I stared at the notification, I was in complete shock, because the very date he was seriously wounded and talking to God in Vietnam when he was nineteen years old, was the exact date that he died, forty years later. I was stunned because I realized the Lord had answered Andrew's prayer that day and granted him precisely forty more years. Forty years to tell the world about Jesus, forty years to get back to me and become my loving husband and live a glorious, blessed life. Forty years to give the twins a beloved father, forty years to have two beautiful daughters, and one stepson, forty years to meet his wonderful grandchildren, forty years to see his children and grandchildren become disciples for the Lord. Forty years to travel the world, and get back to Vietnam. Back to the tunnels, back to the place where the Lord had personally, answered his prayer and extended his life exactly forty years.

I could not get over the fact that the Lord had given Andrew specifically forty years, because the number forty is a very significant number in the Bible. I reached across the table and picked up my Bible and opened it and I read: God commanded Noah to build an ark, and the rains flooded the Earth for 40 days and 40 nights. The Israelites were punished for lacking faith, and they were forced to wander in the wilderness for 40 years before reaching the Promise Land. Moses went on a 40-day fast before he received the Ten Commandments from God. When Jesus was tested by Satan, he fasted for 40 days and 40 nights. Also, 40 writers wrote the Bible. As I read these scriptures,

I realized the number 40 in the Bible seems to be closely associated with times of trial and testing that had led to transformation. The number 40 is connected to the fulfillment of God' promise.

The Hebrew people believed that it took 40 years for a new generation to arrive (Numbers 32:13). Several early Hebrew leaders and kings were said to have ruled for 'forty years,' because that is a generation. I read in my Bible concordance that scripture mentions the number 40, at least 149 times throughout the Bible. It means testing, trials and finally triumph.

Andrew had been my forever love since I first saw him that day in our youth group; when we were only thirteen years old. He was so handsome, polite, and mature. He was honest, intelligent, and composed; he became my best friend, my soulmate, and my prince charming. I loved our life together, and I will never stop thanking the Lord for giving him forty more years, because those were the best years of our life.

Two things change your life forever...Love and Grief. No one's life is perfect, but my life was blessed beyond anything I could have ever imagined, and I am grateful to my Lord every day for giving Andrew those extra forty years, so that we could fulfill our life's love story.

Everyone has a story to tell. The next-time you look across the church, and see a lighthearted old white-haired man or women sitting alone, smiling, and praising the Lord with all their heart, do not mock them...look closer! See their joyful spirit. Maybe they are reverently singing and worshiping God because their lifetime has been so blessed. They may be filled with the joy of the Lord, because they have such an amazing life story to tell.

"There will come a time when every step of the journey God is taking you on will make sense. Until then keep living." *Toby Mac*

1 Thessalonians 5:16-18, Rejoice always, pray continually, give thanks in all circumstances; for this is God's will for you in Christ Jesus.

Made in the USA
Middletown, DE
17 October 2022